WITHDRAWN

THE MOONSTONE
LEGACY

THE MOONSTONE LEGACY

DIANA DE GUNZBURG

TONY WILD

PUSHKIN PRESS
LONDON

This edition first published in 2010 by
Pushkin Press
12 Chester Terrace
London N1 4ND

Reprinted 2010, 2011

British Library Cataloguing in Publication Data:
A catalogue record for this book is available
from the British Library

ISBN 978 1 906548 21 6

Cover: *Sezincote under Moonlight* 2009
© Julian Civiero

Frontispiece: *Shalimar 2009*
© Nesta Fitzgerald

Diana de Gunzburg © Giorgia Fiorio

Tony Wild © Stéphane Perera

Set in 11 on 14.2 Monotype Baskerville MT
and printed in Great Britain on 90 gsm Munken Premium White
by MPG Books Cornwall

www.pushkinpress.com

THE MOONSTONE
LEGACY

By day I gleam, the golden sun of burning cloudless noon;
By night, amid the asterisms I glide, the dappled moon!

Bhagavadgītā Chapter 10
Of Religion by the Heavenly Perfections

1

DEATH BY MOONLIGHT

Blood dripped from Lizzy's hands into the snow. Her mother's blood.

"Mum!" she cried, pleading, clutching her body close, willing her not to die.

"Lizzy!" her mother whispered. Her eyes wide open in terror, gazing at something …

Lizzy turned.

But there was nothing. Just the glimmering dome of Shalimar, the frozen moors beyond and, hanging high in the ice-clear sky, the full moon.

2

THE ANNIVERSARY

IT HAD BEEN TWO YEARS to the day since her mother's death, but the horror of that moment was seared in her memory for ever.

As fourteen-year-old Lizzy stood under the great cedar tree where the accident had happened she laid a bunch of lilies on the ground. Sighing, she brushed a strand of long dark hair from her face as she looked across the sweeping lawns to Shalimar. Its intricate stone arches and pavilions glowed in the last rays of the setting sun. "The Taj Mahal of the Yorkshire moors!" her mother had called it—and promised to take her to see the famous monument one day. But there would be no trip to India, no Taj Mahal …

It was almost dark by the time Lizzy made her way back home to Maya Lodge. She was surprised to find her Uncle William's old Bentley parked outside.

What's he doing here? Lizzy wondered. Uncle William hardly ever came to visit. Her father, who was a scientist, rented the lodge from his elder brother, but he and Aunt Lavinia were usually far too busy hosting fancy shoots, dinners and weekend parties at Shalimar to take much notice of them.

Sitting on the bench under the wooden veranda, Lizzy pulled off her wellies and let herself in. Uncle William's voice was booming from the living room. " … If I were you, Henry, I'd be worried sick about Lizzy," he said. She stopped in her tracks, listening intently. "I don't know how you've coped, I really don't. After Alice's death, I hardly slept, I can tell you. All I could think was that it could be my kids next … "

"Don't be so melodramatic, William," Lizzy heard her father reply. "You can't honestly expect me to still believe that ridiculous curse story Nanny used to frighten us with!"

What the hell's he talking about? Lizzy tiptoed down the narrow hallway and stood stock-still near the half-open door.

"Come on, Henry!" Uncle William said. "You know full well that ever since that no-good George Abercrombie disappeared off the face of the earth, one in every generation of the family has died in some sort of terrible accident. And when did they all die?"

Her father didn't reply. Lizzy could sense the tension between them.

"On the full moon!" Uncle William said. "And unfortunately your wife was no exception. Is it any wonder they say that the Abercrombie family is cursed!"

Oh my God! The full moon! Lizzy flashed back to the moment of her mother's death.

The springs of the armchair squeaked as Uncle William hauled himself to his feet. "Listen, I'm sorry, I really didn't mean to end up arguing with you like this, not today of all days. But just take care of Lizzy, that's all. I'd better get going. In any case, Lavinia's got a houseful of guests, and there'll be hell to pay if I'm late back … "

Lizzy slid unseen into the loo under the stairs as her father accompanied Uncle William down the hall. She leant back against the door, heart pounding.

3

THE TEMPLE OF THE MOON

S HANKAR PUJARI looked down from the top of a rocky hill on the coast of Gujarat in India. Below lay the familiar white marble walls of the Temple of the Moon, the Arabian Sea beyond glistening in the moonlight. Streams of white-robed pilgrims were converging on the temple from all sides for the opening ceremony of the Soma Mela festival.

He nodded to his driver, who went to the boot of the car and got out a large trunk. Shankar changed from his elegant suit into the ochre robes of a Brahmin priest.

"Wait here!" he said, and set off down the stony pathway leading to the Temple.

Minutes later he joined the heaving crowds of pilgrims flooding into the temple. Drums throbbed incessantly, and the stifling heat reeked of sweat and incense. All eyes were fixed on the head Brahmin priest, who swung a censer in front of the statue of the six-armed Moon God. The pilgrims chanted incantations at the sight of the bronze idol gleaming in the light of guttering oil lamps.

As Shankar pushed his way slowly towards the back of the temple he glanced towards the other Brahmins gathered

17

around the statue. He'd been cast out of their priestly brotherhood at the age of fifteen. They said he had violated his oath and had become obsessed.

Obsessed! If they only knew!

As he sat in the dim torchlight of the temple archive, Shankar surveyed the old documents spread in front of him. He frowned, shaking his head. He was no closer to finding what he was looking for.

The frenetic drumming of the ceremony was reaching its climax. *Not much time left.*

Quickly gathering all the papers together, he stuffed them into the satchel he had hidden under his robes. Something fell out of a yellowed envelope—a rusty clasp knife, a tarnished inscription on its silver handle. He breathed on the metal, and polished it on his robe—peering at it closely, a smile began to play across his lips …

"*George Abercrombie,*" he read. "*The Honourable Company Resident, Junagadh, India 1853.*"

4

THE LAST DAY OF TERM

"I'M GOING TO BE LATE for school!" Lizzy shouted to her father, grabbing her rucksack and rushing out of the door of Maya Lodge. "Bye, Dad!"

Slamming it behind her, she ran out into the rain. As she closed the garden gate she spotted Aunt Lavinia's Range Rover swooshing down the drive from Shalimar.

"Stop!" she shouted, waving her arms.

The window opened, and her aunt glared out. "What is it, Lizzy?" she asked. "I'm in a hurry."

"Please! I'm late! I'm going to miss the bus!"

"Typical! Your father just lets you get away with this sort of behaviour time after—"

"Time. I know, I haven't any. Please?"

"Get in the back, then. But be quick about it!"

Lizzy jumped in. "Oh, hello Samuel!" she said, surprised to see her cousin in the passenger seat. He was looking miserable, clutching his jaw. "What's wrong?"

"I've got a rotten toothache," Samuel complained. "First day of the hols and it kept me up all night. We're off to the dentist … "

"Hang on, you two!" her aunt said, putting her foot down. They roared down the long puddled drive and out into the main street of Nethermoorside.

19

The school bus was just about to leave. Aunt Lavinia cut in front, tooting the horn and flapping her hand imperiously out of the window. "I won't do this again, I warn you, young lady!" she said.

The last few schoolchildren were scrambling onboard. "Crikey!" said Samuel, staring at them. "Are those really the sort of yobs you have to go to school with?"

"At least they're not snobs ... " Lizzy muttered to herself, hopping out. "Thanks, Aunt Lavinia!"

She ran over to the bus. "Hi, Josh!" she said, greeting a boy whose parents worked at Shalimar.

"Now then," Josh replied as they clambered onboard. The Range Rover drew away.

"Ooo! Got a chauffeur now, 'ave you, Lizzy?" a girl shouted from the back of the bus.

"Slummin' it a bit with the likes of us, aren't you?" added another girl to rowdy laughter and whistles from a couple of the boys.

"Ignore 'em, Lizzy," Josh said over his shoulder.

"Don't worry," Lizzy told him. "I always do."

As the bus sloshed down the wet, winding lanes towards Knowlesby, everyone eventually calmed down. Lizzy wiped the mist off the rain-splattered window and stared out across the sodden fields, thinking about the curse that her Uncle William had talked about. He'd seemed so sure ...

Drab tinsel hung limply around the walls of the assembly hall of Knowlesby High School. "And finally, I'd like to wish you all a very Happy Christmas!" Hardly had the headmaster finished his end-of-term speech when there was a clattering of chairs as the excited pupils fled for the relative warmth of the classrooms.

The last day of term seemed to drag on for ever. Lizzy's final lesson was Art with the annoying Miss Franklin—she'd been a student of her mother's at York Art School years before, and had even visited Maya Lodge. Miss Franklin floated around the classroom in her tight-fitting jeans and low-cut hippy blouse, everyone's best friend. Pausing for a moment, she bent over the table where Lizzy was mixing her paints, and started to recite a poem quietly:

"Mine eye hath play'd the painter and hath stell'd
Thy beauty's form in table of my heart … "

Lizzy rolled her eyes, really regretting that she'd told Miss Franklin that her father loved Shakespeare's sonnets. It had turned out that she loved them too, and insisted on quoting them at her all the time.

"How is your father, Lizzy?" Miss Franklin asked.

"Fine," Lizzy muttered.

"You must both miss your mother terribly. So hard for you, I'm sure."

When Lizzy didn't respond, Miss Franklin patted her shoulder, and turned to the class. "Right, I'd like you all to do a painting about what Christmas means to you. Let your imagination be your guide … "

Concentrating intently, Lizzy took longer over her picture than anyone else. It was only when the bell went and everyone noisily said their goodbyes that she leant back in her chair, finally taking in what she'd painted.

She swallowed hard, and blinking back a tear, scrumpled it up.

5

HOMECOMING

THE SUN WAS SETTING as the bus drew into Nethermoorside.

As Lizzy got off, a gust of wind ruffled her hair and sent
the last remnants of the autumn leaves skittering past
her down the village street. The clouds to the west were
turning a violent orange; drystone walls criss-crossed
the small fields in the valley and the distant bleating of
sheep filled the dank moorland air.

She walked through the gates and up the oak avenue
through the estate, pausing to look across the park to
Shalimar. Funny—usually she loved everything about
the house, but today she found something sinister and
oppressive in its sinuous oriental curves. She pulled her
coat tight around her and hurried on.

"Hi, Dad!" she shouted from the hallway of Maya
Lodge as she dropped her rucksack and hung up
her coat. "School's over, thank God. No more Miss
Franklin getting on my nerves. I did my Christmas
shopping before I came home. You're going to love
your present."

She put her head round the living room door. Her father was gazing into the fire.

"Don't you want to know what it is?" Lizzy continued.

"What?"

"Your present."

"What present?"

Lizzy shook her head. "Never mind. What do you want for supper?"

"Whatever you like."

"Could we go to the pub or something? You know, for a change."

"I don't think I could take all that jingle-bells nonsense right now."

"I'm going to my room then." There was a slight catch in Lizzy's voice. "I'll make supper later on."

"Okay." Her father stood up and put another log on the fire as Lizzy ran up the stairs. He picked up the last photograph he'd taken of her and her mother together. They were looking directly at the camera, dark eyes flashing, smiling at some silly joke he'd made.

Lizzy had grown to look more and more like Alice in the last two years, he thought. Sometimes he could hardly bring himself to look at her.

A loud knock at the door jolted Henry from his reverie. Sighing, he put the photograph down and went to open it. A good-looking young woman was standing in the porch.

"Mr Abercrombie? I'm so sorry to call by unannounced," she said, her voice low and breathy. "I'm Rose Franklin. Lizzy's art teacher … "

"Oh! Right … " Henry held out his hand. "Pleased to meet you, Miss Franklin. Do come in—I'll get Lizzy." He could hear music blaring in her bedroom.

"No, don't, please," Miss Franklin said, putting her hand on his arm. "It's you I need to talk to."

"Oh, really?" Henry said, taking her coat. "Nothing serious, I hope?"

Miss Franklin gave him a concerned smile as he showed her into the living room. "I've been here once before," she remarked. "Maybe Lizzy told you?" Henry shook his head. "I was pupil of your wife's at York Art College. She invited me for lunch when Lizzy was very young. Alice was a wonderful teacher," she continued as they sat down. "I was so sorry to hear of her death."

"Yes. Thank you," Henry replied stiffly.

"Actually, that's what I've come to talk to you about."

Henry looked at her, momentarily taken aback, but there was something so direct and guileless in her expression that he relaxed.

"Very well," he said.

Miss Franklin refused the drink that he offered her, getting straight to the point. "I've been worried about Lizzy for a while now," she told him. "You know her grades have gone down dramatically and her behaviour is very erratic?" Henry nodded, guiltily remembering the school reports that lay unopened in his desk.

"But it's the painting that she did today that really worries me." Miss Franklin got a rumpled sheet of paper from her handbag, and started to smooth it out on the table. "I read about your wife's death in the newspapers at the time. So you can imagine my reaction when I saw this … "

"My God!" Henry whispered, the colour draining from his face. Lizzy had painted a huge cedar tree framed against a darkening winter sky. A stream of bright-red blood poured from a swollen full moon into the snow below. He slumped back in his chair. "It was two years ago," he said quietly, as if talking to himself. "Alice was working on a whole series of paintings of Shalimar for her exhibition in India. Then my brother asked her to paint one of his wife's horse in front of the house. He offered to pay her for it, and … "

"And?" Miss Franklin encouraged gently.

"And so Alice agreed. Lizzy helped her bring Fire down from the stables and tethered him under one of the cedars in the park for Alice to paint. It had snowed heavily the night before and one of the branches … "—Henry took a deep breath—" … The police said one of the branches of the cedar had snapped off under the weight of snow and must have panicked Fire. He broke free, kicking out and catching Alice a blow on the head. Lizzy found her hours later. She died in her arms."

"How awful!" Miss Franklin whispered.

Henry couldn't take his eyes off Lizzy's painting. "There's something else," he said eventually. "Something I didn't realise Lizzy knew about. The moon … Alice died on the full moon … "

6

TROUBLE WITH THE SAMS

LIZZY TOSSED AND TURNED, dreaming wild dreams about the curse until she was woken by a shaft of sunlight falling on her face. Rubbing her eyes, she got unsteadily out of bed and threw open the window. Cold moorland air flooded in—she shook her head and breathed deeply, looking out onto the rolling parkland running down to the Shalimar lake which glittered in the bright winter sunlight.

Leaning out, she spotted her cousins trotting down the oak-lined driveway, coming back from their morning ride. "Hey, you two!" she shouted, waving. Quickly pulling on her clothes, she ran downstairs and grabbed two apples from the fruit bowl as she rushed outside.

"Hello, cuz," Samuel and Samantha said, halting in front of Maya Lodge. They were dressed in matching tweed jackets, black riding hats and shiny long boots.

"Hello, cuzzes," Lizzy replied, imitating their drawl pitch-perfectly as she fed an apple to each of their beautiful horses and patted their necks. "How's the toothache?"

"Gone," said Samuel. He fiddled with the polished leather reins of Hardy, his perfectly-groomed bay.

"And so's the tooth," added Samantha. "Nice start to the hols." The Sams—as the sixteen-year-old twins were known—were home from Laythorpe College, an expensive boarding school an hour's drive away.

"We only broke up yesterday," Lizzy told them, kissing Hardy on the nose.

"Are you looking forward to the Christmas party season, Lizzy?" Samantha asked.

Samuel butted in before Lizzy could reply. "We've been invited out nearly every night, haven't we, Sammy?" He looked smugly at Samantha, who nodded, tucking a stray blonde lock under her riding hat.

Lizzy always found it creepy how alike the Sams looked. She could never work out whether it was Samantha who was more like a boy or Samuel who was more like a girl, because in appearance they met somewhere in the middle. They were both very good-looking in an icy blond sort of way, and attracted attention wherever they went. Not that they noticed—they were far too wrapped up in each other.

"You're still riding those old nags at Cold Kirby, I suppose?" Samuel said

"Yeah," Lizzy replied. Every Saturday afternoon she cycled to work at the stables in a nearby village; her riding was improving, but unfortunately it was true that the horses there weren't up to much.

"Too bad, eh?" said Samantha. "See you later … "

Lizzy watched enviously as the Sams rode away, and was about to go back into the Lodge when they suddenly turned round and trotted back.

"You know, I just said to Sam you might like to have a ride on Stetson," Samantha told her as they rode up, glancing at Samuel with an odd expression on her face. "Nothing much, just a trot up the lane. So you can feel what it's like to ride a proper horse."

"Wow, that would be great!" Lizzy exclaimed.

"Here you go then!" Samantha slipped off Stetson and handed her the reins.

As Lizzy was scrambling on, Samuel lent over and whacked the horse with his crop, and it charged off. She struggled to stay on as Samuel galloped past, an expression of cruel amusement on his face.

"Bastard!" Lizzy shouted at him fumbling with her foot for the stirrup as he tore ahead.

Racing across Shalimar park, Samuel ducked low as he deliberately rode under the branch of a huge oak. Lizzy hung on, completely out of control. "Ouch!" she cried as a small branch lashed her forehead. Stetson thundered on after Hardy, sailing over a huge log effortlessly. "I'll show you!" she said to herself as Samuel slowed Hardy at the top of the high bank leading down to the lake. Lizzy kicked Stetson on.

"Hey!" Samuel shouted as she flew past him, belting flat-out down the steep slope.

Before she knew it, she was galloping through the shallows of the lake sending up plumes of spray into the bright midday sun. Ducks scattered left and right, quacking and flapping their wings. She raced out of the water onto the lawns sloping up to Shalimar, its great copper dome glinting against the bracken-gold moors beyond. She halted Stetson on the gravel just in front of the high arched entrance, and hopped off, throwing her arms around his neck. "You were brilliant!" she panted in his ear.

Samuel arrived, glowering. "You'll pay for this," he said.

The front doors of Shalimar flew open as Aunt Lavinia barged out, her immaculately tweaked eyebrows quivering. "What on earth do you think you're doing, young lady?" she shouted. "That's Samantha's horse!"

Lizzy could muster no more than an ecstatic grin as her aunt's black labradors tumbled out behind her and started barking at everyone and everything.

"Oh, for God's sake," Lavinia said between clenched teeth. "Skittle ... Ben! Shut up!" They took no notice.

Samantha arrived out of breath, having run directly from Maya Lodge. "I said you could take Stetson for a trot, Lizzy," she puffed, glancing at her mother. "Not a full-scale bloody race!"

"But Samuel whacked him!" Lizzy protested, brought back down to earth with a bump.

"Whacked?" retorted Samuel. "It was just a tap! I hardly even touched him!"

"I'm sure you're right, darling," Aunt Lavinia said, and turned on Lizzy. "You're a reckless, irresponsible girl!"

Uncle William appeared at her side, alerted by the commotion. A red-faced man in his early forties, he was as unlike Lizzy's father as a twin brother could possibly be. "What's going on?" he asked, patting Skittle absently on the head.

"Lizzy took Samantha's horse without her permission," Lavinia told him. "It's ridiculous! Henry's let the girl run positively wild—"

"But ... " Lizzy tried to make herself heard as she wiped the blood from her forehead with the back of her hand.

"Stetson could have been injured!" Aunt Lavinia raged on. "He cost us a fortune! I will not tolerate such behaviour!

TROUBLE WITH THE SAMS

You must take her back to the Lodge at once, William, and tell Henry what his daughter has been up to!"

"Must I?" asked William meekly. But one steely glance from his wife answered him. "Of course … "

"Giddons!" Lavinia bellowed, marching off towards the stable block to find the groom, Skittle hanging off Ben's ear as the labs followed behind. "Where's Giddons?"

Uncle William sighed. "You'd better come with me, Lizzy," he said, walking towards the gleaming Bentley parked nearby. He avoided Lizzy's eye. But then he never looked directly at anyone, his eyes always flitting shiftily from side to side.

As they drove down towards Maya Lodge, he spotted the smear of blood on Lizzy's face. "You're not hurt, I hope?" he asked.

"What? No, it's okay, thanks."

"What was that I heard about Samuel whacking the horse?"

"Whacked! It was just a tap!" Lizzy drawled in reply, imitating her cousin. "I hardly even touched him!"

Uncle William couldn't stop himself chuckling as they drew up outside Maya Lodge.

Lizzy's father was working on some papers and looked up from the table in surprise when his elder twin walked into the sitting room, Lizzy trailing behind.

"Hello, Henry!" William said. "Can't get rid of me these days, you see! I'm afraid I have to report a bit of a rumpus up at the house!"

"Oh … um, hello William. I'm not sure this is a good time—" He caught sight of the blood on his daughter's pale forehead. "Are you okay, Lizzy?"

"Don't worry, it's nothing—I got a cut from a branch," Lizzy explained quickly. "I'll go and clean it up."

"Brave girl," William said as she left. "I'm sure she'll be alright. The thing is Lavinia wanted me to … well, you know what's she's like … " He shrugged hopelessly. "Look here, I could do with a drink … "

"Of course. Sorry," Henry started to get up.

"It's alright, I know where to find it." William lumbered over to the drinks cabinet, pouring himself a large whisky and signalling with the bottle to his brother who shook his head. "Anyway, it's no big deal," William continued, settling himself heavily in an armchair. "Apparently Lizzy took Samantha's horse for a flat-out gallop when she only said she could take him for a trot. And he hit him with a stick. Samuel that is. Or something like that. It all seems a bit of a storm in a teacup to me, but Lavinia's hopping mad and she's sent me to complain about it to you … "

"Ah," Henry said.

"Listen, I've got an idea … Why don't I tell Lavinia that you were livid with Lizzy and threatened to ground her for the holidays? That should satisfy her … "

Henry nodded. "If you like … "

William hadn't noticed how exhausted his brother looked in the dim light of that previous evening. But now he could see how his face was thin and drawn and his thick brown hair shot through with grey. "Look, I'm sorry if I got a bit carried away yesterday," William said.

"Don't worry about it," Henry replied. "If in doubt, blame that stupid nanny of ours. What was she called?"

"I only remember her as Nanny," William said. "She did succeed in terrifying us, though, didn't she?"

Lizzy appeared in the open doorway, dabbing her head with kitchen roll.

"Do you need something, Lizzy?" her father asked.

"Have we got any disinfectant?" Lizzy said.

"Look in the medicine cabinet. Downstairs loo." Her father waved vaguely.

William downed his drink. "Got to go. Promised Rupert Shotley I'd show him around the estate this morning. Remember what I said about grounding Lizzy, old boy!" He caught sight of Lizzy standing in the hallway clutching a pad of cotton wool to her head. "Don't worry, my dear, it's just me and your father conspiring to pull the proverbial over the eyes of She-Who-Must-Be-Obeyed."

As he followed Uncle William into the hallway, her father suddenly exclaimed, "Mabel Corker! That was our nanny's name!"

Uncle William stopped as if he'd run slap bang into an invisible wall. "Oh, really?" Lizzy watched as Uncle William turned slowly, looking steadily at her father, holding his eye. "I don't remember."

He was lying. Lizzy could tell.

7

SNOW

8

"ARE YOU ALL RIGHT, luv?" Annie Peckitt asked the next day. Lizzy was standing with a bauble for the Christmas tree in hand, looking as if she didn't quite remember what she was supposed to be doing with it.

"What? Oh, yeah ... " Lizzy hung it from the small tree that they were decorating together. Annie came to Maya Lodge once a week from Knowlesby to help with the cleaning, and Lizzy had known her for ever. She wished she could ask her if she'd heard of the curse, but she didn't want her father to find out that she knew about it.

"Are you sure, luv?" Annie asked again as she wound a length of silver tinsel round the tree. "It's just you don't seem yerself."

"No, honest, Annie, I'm fine, thanks." Lizzy stood on a stool and put the star at the top of the tree.

"That finishes it off right nice." Annie said. She glanced out of the window. "Oh look, luv! I'd best get a move on—the snow's settling thick and fast!" She went through to the hall and put on her coat. "I wouldn't want to get stuck 'ere all Christmas. My Ron would make a right pig's ear of the turkey."

"Happy Christmas!" Lizzy escorted her to the door. "And love to all your family!"

35

"And to you, luv." Annie hugged her warmly and kissed her on both cheeks. "You're sure you're alright, mind?"

"I'm fine," Lizzy replied. "Drive safely."

After she'd gone Lizzy stoked up the fire and sat on the window seat, looking out of the window absently as the familiar landscape was transformed by the blizzard. The black silhouettes of the branches of the trees acquired a white shadow of snow, and the green fields were covered with a pristine tablecloth.

She caught sight of hooded figure struggling up the driveway on a mountain bike, a dog scampering alongside him.

She jumped up and ran outside.

"Hello, Josh!" she called just as he rode past the Lodge gate. As he turned in surprise the bike skidded and he ended up falling in a tangle in the snow.

Lizzy burst out laughing—he looked ridiculous lying on his back like an upturned turtle, his face flushed from his exertions.

"Why don't you push the bike?" she said. "You won't get far trying to ride it."

Josh struggled to his feet, catching his breath. "I've only got me trainers on and they'd get soaked."

"I'll lend you some wellies and help you push it if you like. I'll just get my coat."

She returned a minute later handing him an old pair of her dad's wellies. "Here you go."

She sat on the bench next to him. "Have you come from the village?"

"Yeah," he answered. "I were at Pete Thompson's, 'aving a guitar lesson. I'm hoping to get one for Christmas."

"I haven't a clue what I'm getting!" Lizzy said, patting his Springer spaniel, who looked up at her, wagging his tail.

36

"Benjy likes you," Josh observed.

"He's obviously got excellent taste!"

"Yeah, just like his master."

Lizzy grinned. There was a pause.

"Me dad mentioned that business about you and the 'orses."

"Yeah, it was brilliant!"

"Me dad taught me to ride when 'e were groom at Levens Hall. I used to exercise the 'orses there sometimes. He says mebbe I can do the same 'ere."

"Lucky you! I've dreamt of riding up on the moors, but the horses at Cold Kirby are too far away, and there's no way Lavinia or the Sams will let me ride theirs."

"C'mon, I've got to get this bike back." Josh picked it up and tied his trainers onto the crossbar. Then he pushed it along with Lizzy giving a hand when the wheels got too gummed up.

As Benjy trotted alongside, his legs disappearing in the snow, they spotted Shalimar through the bare trees.

"It's great, that Indian style, isn't it?" Josh said. His parents had only started working at Shalimar in the autumn, and he still found it new and exciting. "Stable Cottage is like that too. I've got my bedroom in the tower. It's really cool."

"Yeah. My great-great-great-grandfather worked in India for years," Lizzy said. "When Uncle George came back he rebuilt the house like an Indian temple to remind him of his time there."

"Uncle George? … "

"That's what we all call him. Anyway, you won't believe it, but after all the work he'd done on the house and gardens and everything, Uncle George suddenly disappeared!"

37

" 'E disappeared?"

"Yeah. Just vanished and he was never heard of again."

"Wow!"

They carried on in silence for a while. The driveway to Stable Cottage wound through woodland around the back of Shalimar, and when they arrived at Josh's house he put the bike in a shed with a sigh of relief.

"Thanks, Lizzy. I wouldn't 'ave fancied riding it all the way."

"It's getting dark," Lizzy said. "I'd better be getting back … "

8

ROSE

A s LIZZY WALKED up to Maya Lodge in the twilight, a rather tatty little silver Fiat drew up outside. To her surprise Miss Franklin got out.

Now what's she doing? Lizzy wondered. Surely she couldn't have anything else to talk to her father about? He'd mentioned Miss Franklin's visit of the previous day, telling Lizzy vaguely that they'd chatted about something to do with school.

"Hello, Miss Franklin," she said politely.

"Hi, Lizzy!" Rose beamed. "I'm going away for Christmas, so I thought I'd bring you a present." Rose scrambled in the back and produced a parcel untidily wrapped in gift paper.

"Oh, thank you!" Lizzy was pleased in spite of herself. "Did you come all the way from Knowlesby specially?"

"It may look ready for the scrap heap," she said, nodding at her car. "But at least it's got four-wheel drive. I sailed past about twenty other cars stuck on the hills."

"Are you going to your parents' for Christmas?" Lizzy asked they walked up the path together.

"My Dad died when I was young, and my mother hasn't spoken to me in years. I'm going to stay with my aunt in London."

9

The door of the Lodge opened and light spilled onto the veranda as Lizzy's father appeared. "I heard a car—" he started to say.

"She's come specially from Knowlesby with a present for me, Dad." Lizzy told him

"That's very kind of you, Miss Franklin," Henry said, looking across the fields. "It's like a different world out here, isn't it?"

"*Beauty o'ersnow'd ...* " Miss Franklin murmured, quoting from one of Shakespeare's sonnets.

" *... and bareness every where.*" Henry completed the line, looking at her in surprise. "You know the sonnets then, Miss Franklin?"

"My favourite poetry. After all, Shakespeare did write about me ... "

Henry frowned, momentarily baffled.

"*A rose by any other name ...* " she started.

" *... would smell as sweet.*" Henry finished.

Their eyes met for an instant.

"You must come in for a drink."

"Thanks," Miss Franklin replied with a regretful smile, "but I'm running late as it is with this blizzard."

"Well, thank you once more and Happy Christmas," Henry said.

"And Happy Christmas to you both, too. Bye, Lizzy."

"Goodbye, Miss Franklin. And thank you so much."

"Rose, remember." She waved her finger with mock severity at Lizzy, who felt impelled to give in.

"Sorry," Lizzy said quickly. "Goodbye, Rose."

9

CHRISTMAS AT SHALIMAR

O N CHRISTMAS MORNING Lizzy sat curled up in the window seat with her book, waiting for her father to come down so that they could go to Shalimar for lunch. She was having trouble getting into *The Lifeline*, the huge best-seller by the famous Indian author Shankar Pujari. She didn't like it all that much—every time one of the main characters had a problem they always found a magical solution. *Life isn't really like that*, she thought, putting it down impatiently and staring out of the window.

It certainly was a properly white Christmas. The snow was a good foot deep in the Lodge garden, and some drifts had built up almost to the levels of the drystone walls in the fields. All the roads to Nethermoorside were blocked—it was reckoned that the village would be cut off from the outside world until after Boxing Day.

Her father came downstairs, wearing a slightly smarter tweed jacket than usual. "So, are you ready for the family's ritual slaughter?" he joked, and Lizzy sensed that he was making a great effort to be cheerful. She wore a new pair of jeans and a short corduroy jacket. Although the snowplough had been up and down the drive a couple of times it was still too treacherous to take their car. So they dressed up warmly and set off on foot.

Her father carried the bag with their shoes and the presents as they walked out of the garden gate and onto the drive. The wind had dropped, and a heavy mist lay over the landscape, muffling their senses—neither sights, nor sounds, nor smells could penetrate its cold embrace.

After trudging through the snow across the park, they crossed the bridge over the stream running through the Indian garden. It was decorated with four lead sculptures of Brahmin bulls, the kind of humped cattle found in India. Two lay on each of the stone parapets gazing placidly at each other. Lizzy cleared the blanket of snow off their backs with her gloved hands.

Downstream, the bridge overlooked the Snake Pool, where the sculpture of a three-headed snake lurked. The heads were sheathed in a skin of ice, and the water of the pond was frozen, trapping the reeds in its glassy grip.

Even though she had seen the sculpture so often, it still gave Lizzy a thrill of horror. She was terrified of snakes—once, when she was five, her mother had taken her to Shalimar to play with the Sams and they'd locked her in an attic room. It had been almost dark, and she was frightened out of her wits when she saw the huge stuffed python Uncle George had brought back from India. It was attached to the wall in horribly lifelike curves, its mouth open and fangs ready to strike. When Aunt Lavinia eventually heard her screams, she'd been shaking so hard she'd been unable to speak.

As she stood looking at the Indian garden, Lizzy remembered what it was like when the weather was warm, with its rushing stream and gigantic plants …

"You know, in summer it's just like *The Lifeline* here, Dad."

"What's that?" her father asked.

"My book. There's a girl called Sita in it. She has to escape from the baddies by wading down a river through a gorge, and she shelters from the rain under a huge leaf just like that umbrella plant—you see, the one just below the pond there? She catches a wild horse at the bottom and gallops off along the valley to alert the others of the danger."

"You and your galloping!" Her father looked at Lizzy fondly and, for the first time in months, smiled.

They rounded the corner at the top of the slope near Shalimar and stopped in their tracks when they saw the house. Through the mist it appeared as if it were a colossal wedding cake. Long icicles hung off the green copper dome, and the wind had sculpted the snow along the line of the roof into great loops. The elaborate window arches were fretted with ice, and around the vast Indian arch above the front door fairy lights shone vainly, their bright colours muted by the mist. Shalimar seemed to hang in space like a still, dreamlike vision on a cloud.

"I've never seen it looking like this before," Lizzy's father said. "It's out of this world."

The front door opened. Tindy Postlethwaite, the housekeeper, was leaving for her sister's house in the village. Her thin lips pursed disapprovingly.

"You'll be wanting to take those boots off, no doubt," Mrs Postlethwaite said without a word of welcome.

"Yes, thank you very much indeed, Mrs P. And a happy Christmas to you, too!" Henry replied with the exaggerated courtesy he used to combat bad manners.

Mrs Postlethwaite didn't notice.

"Might be for them that doesn't have work to do later," she said, "or for some that like to make work for others by trailing their muck around!" She glared at Lizzy who had brought in a couple of lumps of snow on her wellies.

You'll get no apology from me, you old dragon! Lizzy thought.

Mrs Postlethwaite walked away down the drive, leaving them standing in the hallway unannounced.

They could hear raised voices from the stairway. "It's only us!" Lizzy shouted, and Samantha came running into the hall, her face flushed with anger. She skidded to a halt when she saw Lizzy and Henry and ran straight back out again.

"Full of festive fun as usual … " her father muttered, sitting down to take off his boots. Lizzy slipped on her new leather trainers. Samantha's rudeness wasn't unexpected—the Sams had never liked Lizzy, and they barely tolerated her father either.

In the entrance hall hung lots of large oil paintings of Shalimar commissioned by Uncle George. Lizzy looked at the one that showed the delicate colonnades of the great curved conservatories on either side of the house. The one on the right didn't exist any more—it had collapsed in a great storm many years before, killing Lionel Abercrombie.

There were more mutterings and shushes, then William, the household's diplomat, arrived into the hall to greet them.

"Hello Lizzy! Hello Henry! Happy Christmas to you both!" He kissed her, and Lizzy winced at the sour smell of whisky on his breath.

Clattering noises came from the kitchen buried deep in the back of the house, and Lavinia could be heard shouting at someone.

"We've only got Maud Batty helping us today," William said as they walked past the huge staircase. "It's her first time."

"God help her!" Lizzy's father murmured, as Lavinia's voice notched up a few decibels.

"Where are Skittle and Ben?" Lizzy asked.

"Locked up in the kennels," William said. "Lavinia says they're too messy."

Lizzy looked up at the first landing as she always did when she came to Shalimar. There hung her favourite painting of all—a full-length portrait of her Uncle George. He cut quite a dash, dressed in a long yellow-silk tunic embroidered with gold thread over floppy black-leather boots, and wearing a curved sword tucked into the red sash around his waist. His blue eyes gazed over his handlebar moustache, and he wore a black turban held together by a silver brooch pinned to the front.

"Lavinia's got a surprise for us," William said as she joined them. "Haven't you my sweet?"

Lavinia smiled mysteriously and led them through to the Durbar Hall.

10

THE DURBAR HALL

S HALIMAR WAS FULL OF silk wall hangings, exquisite
Mughal miniatures, vast ebony cabinets inlaid with
mother-of-pearl, ivory dressing tables and huge murals
of Indian scenes. But the Durbar Hall was where Uncle
George had evidently decided he could unleash the full
flood of his passion for his Indian theme. He used to enter-
tain the local farmers and squires there, sitting on a Persian
rug and puffing on his silver water pipe. What they made of
him Lizzy could only guess, but of all the rooms in the house
the Durbar Hall was her favourite.

Her father had told Lizzy that a 'durbar' was the Indian
word for a meeting involving an emperor, or a maharajah,
and their courtiers. Every palace had a magnificent room
which was set aside for such meetings, he'd said—the
durbar hall. Having seen a few in India, Uncle George had
decided to build his version of a durbar hall in Yorkshire.

William threw open the mahogany double doors
leading into the Hall, sang out loudly "Da Dum!" and
ceremoniously bowed Lizzy and Henry in.

"Wow!" Lizzy exclaimed.

Above the middle of the marble floor was a glimmering
stainless-steel candelabra, like a huge cartwheel flipped on

its side, bright with the light of a hundred candles. Each one was flanked by a long sculpted steel flame which curled and flared upwards, sending shards of candlelight darting everywhere. The candelabra was held up by four strong chains that converged on the glass roof high above.

"Of course, we're lucky to see it when the candles are lit so you get the full effect," Lavinia announced. "Rajesh Jog, the sculptor … "—she paused to allow Henry to appreciate the fact that none other than the celebrated Rajesh Jog had made the candelabra—" … he says that without candlelight it is like the sun on a cloudy day."

The candelabra made the Durbar Hall look even more spectacular than usual. The carved marble pillars and arches inlaid with jade and lapis lazuli gleamed in the dappled candlelight, which made the intricate grey-and-white patterns of the marble floor swirl like miniature armies on manoeuvre, and gave the Indian swords, shields and armour hung high up on the walls a new, mysterious glow. The delicate pierced marble screens flickered in an ever-changing play of shadow and light.

Halfway along one wall was a huge marble fireplace in which oak logs were burning, and at the far end there was an enormous Christmas tree. It was covered with tiny white pinprick lights reaching right to its top only a few feet below the glass roof. There were no other decorations, and the tree looked simply beautiful. Tastefully wrapped presents were arranged artfully around its base.

William looked around appreciatively. "Lavinia, my love, you've excelled yourself this year."

Lavinia looked pleased. Every Christmas she tried to improve the decorations, but she found it increasingly difficult to come up with new ideas. The candelabra was one of her more inspired ones, but it had been hideously expensive and even the ever-obliging William had recoiled when he heard what it would cost. She couldn't wait to show it off at the next Shalimar Midsummer Ball.

"William! Do go and fetch the Sams. Christmas isn't Christmas unless we're all together."

While William trotted away obediently, Lizzy steeled herself and walked over to the fireplace. Above the mantelpiece hung the picture of Fire that her mother had been finishing when she died. Lizzy had always avoided looking at it before, but she knew that, sooner or later, she'd have to … have to face up to it. But as soon as she looked, she recoiled, wishing she hadn't—her mother had painted the full moon hanging over the dome of Shalimar, an eerie reminder of her own painting. Lizzy turned away.

William reappeared, ushering the Sams forward like a sheepdog. They were both dressed in oyster-grey cord jeans and matching grey cashmere sweaters. Samantha had drawn her platinum blonde hair back in a neat little bun—she would have been beautiful if she hadn't looked so foul-tempered. Samuel's hair was cut fashionably short, and while he didn't look quite as sour as Samantha, his good looks were marred by the sneer which loitered permanently on his top lip.

"Happy Christmas!" The Sams looked as if the seasonal greeting had had to be dragged out of them under torture.

"And Merry Christmas to you two, too," Henry replied, making an effort to be amusing.

The Sams rolled their eyes. It was an old joke, and a worn one.

"Is Peregrine coming?" Lizzy asked her aunt, trying to put the painting out of her mind.

49

"No, he won't be with us this year, I'm afraid," Lavinia said. She didn't get on with the family's most inscrutable relative, and only ever asked him out of a sense of obligation. "You know what he's like … "

"Oh well, all the more for us," Uncle William joked, secretly relieved that he wasn't coming, too. Since boyhood both he and Henry had been in awe of their brilliant younger cousin.

They all sat down on the Persian rug under the Christmas tree, and William politely started to hand round presents. The Sams complained loudly about almost every one of the many gifts they received. Lavinia herself wasn't much better; she looked at the presents that William gave her as if she were weighing up what she could swap them for when she next went down to London.

Her father gave Lizzy a red polo-neck sweater and the latest Heart 2 Heart CD, and she gave him some of his favourite aftershave. Rose had given her a copy of *The Lifeline*, which of course she already had. She got a book token from the Sams—Lizzy was sure that Aunt Lavinia had forged their handwriting because the greeting inside was surprisingly friendly. Aunt Lavinia and Uncle William gave her a copy of the same CD that they'd given her for her birthday and which she didn't like anyway. Henry was given some soap—it looked suspiciously like the soap that Lavinia had been given by someone the previous year, and had complained to Lizzy about. The Sams hardly even bothered to look at the board game that Lizzy gave them.

Nonetheless, in the end everybody managed to thank everybody else for their presents as if they meant it, and Maud Batty was summoned to collect up the wrapping paper. She was a plain, heavy, pink-faced girl who had only recently come to work at Shalimar.

"Doesn't Maud have family to go to for Christmas?" Henry asked as she left.

"Oh, no," said Lavinia. "She came here from St Andrew's, the children's home in Knowlesby. It's better if staff don't have family, I find—it keeps them more loyal."

Lizzy glared at her aunt, outraged. She talked about Maud as if she weren't a proper person at all.

"Right, let's go to table, everybody," Lavinia said, oblivious.

As there were only six of them, they didn't use the dining room, which had an enormous table, big enough for a banquet. Instead, a round polished oak table had been set up under the new candelabra. Lavinia being Lavinia, it had been beautifully laid with gleaming silver and starched linen napkins. Even as they sat down she couldn't resist straightening a fork in Henry's setting that was a millimetre out of place.

Small crystal glass bowls had already been laid on the place mats. "We have a *delice* of prawn and spinach to start," announced Lavinia. "Maud, hand around the toasts, would you?" Maud shuffled awkwardly round the table with a basket full of perfect triangles of toasted brown bread.

Toasts? thought Lizzy, suppressing a giggle as she took one. She'd only ever had toast before. "I know a Delice," she told her aunt. "Delice Tasker. She's always on the school bus. She looks a bit like a prawn."

Lavinia affected not to hear; it was not her idea of elevated conversation. "Pour the white wine, Maud."

Maud, who had only been taught how to serve wine that morning, was terrified of doing it wrong. By the time she had brought it from the ice bucket she was trembling so much that she missed William's glass, and some wine splashed onto the table.

Lavinia's look could have cut diamonds. Even her immaculately coifed platinum hair acquired a menacing glare.

"You stupid idiot," she hissed. "I showed you exactly how to serve it!"

The Sams chortled at Maud's evident distress.

"It's all right, Lavinia, my love," William said, dabbing the wet patch with his napkin. "There's plenty more where that came from."

Lavinia looked at him in despair. "That's not the point, William. The whole wine cellar could be bursting with bottles for all I care. I am trying to maintain standards."

William had taken a large mouthful of toast with the *delice* spread on top.

"And so you do, my sw—" he stopped, spluttering, as a crumb went down the wrong way. Lizzy thumped him on the back as he coughed and wheezed, and then he sneezed a huge sneeze of mangled toasts and *delice*, clutching his napkin to his nose as it was the nearest thing to hand.

"There, that's better now … " He dried his eyes and spread his napkin back over his knees.

Lavinia stared at William in disgust. Henry looked at the candelabra and whistled tunelessly between his teeth. The Sams sniggered unpleasantly.

Lizzy felt an inarticulate rage boiling up inside her. The whole scene was grotesque—she felt like shaking everyone until their heads dropped off.

"Maud, get Mr Abercrombie a fresh napkin, would you?" Lavinia ordered, her hard blue eyes not leaving William's face for an instant.

It's going to be long meal … Lizzy thought.

11

BAD BEHAVIOUR

AND IT PROBABLY WOULD have been, had not William started talking about the candelabra just as they had nearly finished eating the turkey.

Although he hadn't been very lively after his choking fit, William recovered his good humour as the wine circulated, and he cleared his plate of his second helping.

He leant back heavily in his chair, and his mildewy eyes inevitably travelled up to the candelabra.

"So, what do you think of it, Henry?" he asked his brother, signalling above him with a swift jab of his head.

"It's good." Henry had been examining it dispiritedly all through the meal. It was easier than trying to make conversation. "I'm an admirer of Rajesh Jog. He seems to have an instinctive grasp of natural forms."

"Well, his wife's drop-dead gorgeous, if that's what you mean … " William chuckled. "I'll tell you something else though, Henry—he's got an instinctive grasp of business. You should have seen what I had to pay for it!"

"I'm sure Henry doesn't want to know, William," Lavinia interrupted. Her voice softened. "Although I must say it was the sweetest present I've ever had. Better even than last year's necklace." She gave William something approximating a loving look, and blew him a kiss.

"And what about the year before that, my sweet?" William refilled his glass, and Lavinia kicked him under the table.

"William … "

"Go on, darling, what was it?" he insisted, while Lavinia tried to silence him with a look. "Well, even if you can't remember, I can! It was the portrait of Fire … " He pointed unsteadily in the direction of the mantelpiece.

His voice trailed off. There was an embarrassed silence for a moment.

"Yes, well, thank you, William," Lavinia said smoothly. "Lizzy, dear, do have some more turkey. Maud, give Lizzy some more … "

There was an edge of panic in Lavinia's voice as Henry slumped in his chair. Lizzy watched her father, appalled. Before her very eyes he seemed to be sinking hopelessly into a quicksand; his face took on that haunted look she'd seen so often.

"Stop it, Dad," Lizzy pleaded. "It's Christmas!"

She looked around the table—the Sams were watching her father closely, relishing the prospect of him behaving strangely; Uncle William was embarrassed by his own tactlessness, and Aunt Lavinia was trying desperately to be the perfect hostess by pretending nothing was wrong.

Something inside Lizzy snapped. It was as if a spark had landed on dry tinder—rage swept through her.

"You're pathetic and selfish!" she shouted at her father. "I lost my mother! Can you imagine what that feels like? There isn't a day I don't think of her! All you think of is yourself, and how much you hurt! What about me?!" Her dark eyes flashed angrily.

The Sams snorted with derision, and Lizzy turned on them.

"Look at you two spoilt little brats! You haven't got an ounce of feeling for anyone except each other!"

"Lizzy! How dare you!" Lavinia exclaimed.

"How dare I what! Criticise your foul, faultless children? You don't care about anything as long as the silver's polished and you've got Maud to kick around."

Maud dropped a tray, and fled from the hall. The Sams both collapsed in giggles. Lavinia rounded on them in fury.

"Samuel! Samantha! How could you let her insult me?"

"Don't be such a bore, Mother … " Samuel's top lip curled in his trademark sneer.

"How dare you speak to me like that?" Lavinia's voice trembled with fury. "William! Do something!"

William shrugged his shoulders hopelessly. Lizzy looked at him with utter contempt.

"William! Do something!" Lizzy mimicked Lavinia. "That'll be the day." She swept the table with her gaze. "You're all pathetic freaks! Pathetic!" She stood up and threw her napkin on the floor. "I've had it. I'm going!"

"Lizzy! Don't!" her father pleaded.

"What? Do you want me to stay and watch you staring into space as usual? You don't think I've had enough of that already? No thank you!" Lizzy turned on her heels and stormed out of the Durbar Hall.

She slammed the heavy mahogany doors behind her.

" … *She makes and unmakes many worlds, and can draw the moon from heaven with a scarlet thread.*" Henry quoted Oscar Wilde quietly to himself, a faraway look in his green eyes.

"What is it with you and the moon, Henry?" Lavinia asked him. "Are you turning into a werewolf?" Her mocking laugh echoed around the marble hall.

The Sams immediately started to howl in unison, and convulsed themselves in sniggers. Henry clutched his head between his hands.

William stood up abruptly, throwing his clean napkin to the ground. "Stop that right away, you two!" he bellowed, infuriated.

The Sams stopped, stunned—they had never heard their father shout before.

"Well, if Lizzy's allowed to go, I'm going too!" announced Samantha after a moment's hesitation. "We didn't want to come in the first place, it was only 'cause you forced us," she said, looking accusingly at her mother and standing up.

"Yah," said Samuel, joining her. "C'mon Sammy, let's go and try out Poisoned Pyramid. Even if it is the old version," he glared at his father. They both left, giggling snidely.

"Samuel! Samantha! Come here this instant!" Lavinia ordered, but her voice had lost its steel, and all of a sudden her face seemed to fracture like a shattered windscreen.

Her voice trembled and tears appeared in her eyes. "If you'll excuse me, Henry," she sniffed, "I have a headache. I need to lie down for a while." She stood up unsteadily, and followed the Sams out of the hall, her heels clicking on the cold marble.

William looked at Henry, whose face was drained of all emotion.

"Well, Henry, I think we should congratulate ourselves on an all-round vintage Abercrombie performance. I'd say a drop of port is called for. Urgently." He lumbered over to the sideboard, picked up a decanter and two glasses, then came back and poured them both a generous measure.

"She's right … " Henry said faintly.

"Who's right, old boy?"

"Lizzy. I've been wrapped up in myself since Alice's death—I've hardly noticed what she's thought or felt."

"Don't be hard on yourself, Henry. God knows, you've been through a rough time."

"But how much rougher has it been for Lizzy? She lost her mother!"

William carefully cut a cigar, and lit it with a long match.

"Her art teacher came round the other day," Henry continued. "She showed me a picture Lizzy had done. It was … disturbing, to say the least. She's obviously haunted by the circumstances of Alice's death. She'd even included the full moon … "

William looked up. "Well, there you go!"

"No, there I definitely do not go, William!" Henry said sharply. "The curse is your obsession, not mine." But even as he said it, he realised that it wasn't true.

"Hmmph!" muttered William.

A veil of silence descended between the two brothers. It was rare that they talked seriously, and now both were thinking their own private thoughts.

After a few minutes Henry looked around him. "Is there a phone in here, William? I must call home and talk to Lizzy."

William put his hand on his brother's arm. "My advice—for what it's worth—is give her some space. She'll still be upset, and you might just make it worse. Believe me, I have had enough experience of tantrums in this household … " He raised his eyes to the ceiling.

"Do you think so?" Henry asked sceptically. He usually didn't take much notice of his elder brother's advice.

"I know so," William reassured him.

12

FULL MOON

"JOSH!" Lizzy whispered, her breath steaming in the cold as she tiptoed into the Shalimar stables at midnight.

"I'm 'ere," he replied. He stepped into a shaft of moonlight, his eyes shining with anticipation. He'd agreed to meet her without knowing what she had in mind, but she'd said to dress up warmly and to leave Benjy at home.

When she had left Shalimar after the row in the Durbar Hall, Lizzy had walked without thinking to Stable Cottage. It had been snowing, and she had stood for a few minutes with her face pressed to the window. The sight of the Giddons family sat around the lunch table with paper hats, laughing and pulling crackers while Benjy slept peacefully in front of the fire had been too much. Josh had glimpsed her as she'd turned away. He'd run after her and asked what was wrong, but all she'd told him was that he had to meet her that night without saying why.

Then Lizzy had gone straight back to Maya Lodge and put on an old Heart 2 Heart CD at full volume in her room. Her father returned shortly after, made sure she was all right, but then left her to her own devices. Lizzy had been in no mood for family discussions. He'd gone to bed early, and it had been easy for her to sneak out.

"So what are we doing 'ere?" Josh asked.

"We're going up on the moor. On Stetson and Hardy. It'll be brilliant! You know I've always dreamt of it, Josh. Don't let me down!"

"But ... " Josh knew he couldn't refuse her even if he had wanted to. It might be risky, but it would be thrilling.

As quietly as they could they tacked the horses up.

Time to go.

The thick snow muffled the sound of the horses' hooves as they led them from the courtyard and back past Stable Cottage.

Breathing a sigh of relief as they mounted, Lizzy looked around properly for the first time. The fog of the day had evaporated, and the full moon hung high in the clear sky, bathing the glittering snow on the moor above them in its brilliant, silvery light. It was almost supernaturally still, as though all creatures except themselves had been suspended motionless by a spell.

It was up to Lizzy to show Josh the way.

She followed a track around the back of Shalimar to the top of the Indian Garden. The moonlight glinted on the ice of the Temple Pond. Josh opened the gate leading from the garden without dismounting.

He's not a bad rider, Lizzy thought as she watched. She liked the way he did things so unobtrusively that you wouldn't necessarily notice he was any good at them.

They trotted up a track into the woods. Now that they were far from the houses they could have talked normally, but something made Lizzy keep her voice low.

"This is the old carriage road my great-great-great-grandmother Penelope built so that even when she was very old she could go to Grimstone Scar."

"Where's that?" Josh whispered back.

"All the way up on the moor, just off the Drove Road. You'll see."

Majestic centuries-old beech trees soared above them as they picked their way up the snowy track that clung onto the flank of a steep valley. At the bottom, icy Eden Beck rushed down through great boulders on its way to the Indian Garden. Fronds of ferns had been frozen into immobility and even the softest moss crunched under the horses' hooves.

They skidded on the thick bed of fallen leaves as they climbed higher and higher, skirting crags along the narrowing valley walls. Icicles hung off the cliffs, and the rushing beck got ever closer. Glades of Scots pines, their straight black trunks disappearing into the canopy of branches high above, replaced the last stands of beech trees.

Lizzy pointed out a foaming rock pool under a waterfall. "You won't believe it, but I come swimming here in summer!"

Josh looked into the dark, swirling water and grimaced. "You're right, I don't."

As they approached the top the track flattened. Up here the beck was just a gently meandering stream. Tufts of spiky marsh grass poked through the thick snow glistening in the moonlight.

They followed the track as it climbed out of the little valley and paused by a gate at the top. They looked down towards Shalimar far below.

"Why did your grandmother build a road all the way up 'ere?" asked Josh in amazement.

"She used to come to Grimstone Scar when she was a kid with my Uncle George," Lizzy explained. "She married

61

him when he came back from India. After he disappeared she used to come here all the time to remember him."

She jumped off Stetson and pushed a gate open. On the other side of the wall the ancient drove road led towards Grimstone Scar. There was no sign that anyone had been on the moor for days. The wind-blown snow lay in great sheets across the wide expanse of the track—it wasn't a road as such, more a clear avenue between the heather on one side and the drystone wall on the other. Under the snow Lizzy knew there lay grass, close-cropped by sheep, as smooth as a well-tended lawn.

"We're mad to be out on a night like this," Josh complained good-humouredly as he clapped his hands together to warm them

"Yes we are! But it's absolutely beautiful!"

13

ON THE MOORS

LIZZY REMOUNTED.

"Let's go!" Like her, Stetson was quivering in anticipation. She kicked him straight into a gallop, and Josh followed her. In an instant they were flying through the moonlit night, the horses' hooves sending great spumes of powdery snow into the star-strewn sky.

"Yeeeeeesss!" Lizzy yelled, elated. The cold air stung her eyes and froze her nose, but she hardly noticed.

Eden Great Moor stretched out in front of them, a vast desert of snow. The moonlight was so bright and the air so clear that they could see other great frozen moors beyond it against the night sky.

Lizzy galloped along the drove road for what seemed like miles until she felt that Stetson could gallop no more and gradually slowed him down, then halted. Lizzy was panting with the sheer exhilaration of the ride. It was only then that she noticed that Josh was trailing far behind. It took him several minutes to catch up.

"What were you playing at, Lizzy?" he glowered at her. "We said we'd stick together and you went off like a bat out of hell."

"Wasn't that just fantastic?" Lizzy enthused, ignoring his concerns. She could tell that he secretly was almost as exhilarated by the ride as she was. "Well, at least we're here, anyway."

Around them towered vast piles of huge boulders, sculpted by aeons of wind and rain into fantastic shapes and stacked on top of one another like the handiwork of a giant. Stunted oaks had wrapped their roots around the bare, black rocks and the flaking bark of silver birches twitched in the still, cold air.

"Is this Grimstone Scar?" Josh asked, awe-struck. "Spooky, isn't it?"

"Let's tie the horses up, and then I'll show you something really spooky!" Lizzy said.

They walked together through the snow-covered bracken, and then without warning Lizzy disappeared into the crack between two huge boulders. They looked as if they had been cleaved from one rock by the blow of a colossal sword. Josh followed her, squeezing through the gap until he came out of the other side.

Lizzy stood stock-still a yard in front of him, gazing into the centre of a natural amphitheatre surrounded by huge rocks. The moonlight shone down from high in the sky, hard and unrelenting, lighting everything with an otherworldly brilliance.

There was no one to be seen. It was like an empty stage set from which an actor had just made his exit. The silence was so intense that they could hear their hearts beating.

"They call this the Sanctuary," Lizzy whispered. "They say that druids used to make sacrifices here … "

"Look there!" Josh said, pointing to where someone had trampled the snow to make a large circle and, just before completing it, had formed a corridor leading to a much smaller circle inside.

"Who could have done that?" Lizzy whispered. "There aren't even any footsteps leading to it … "

"Weird!" Josh said quietly. "And I know that shape. It's a really old sign called the cup and ring. You find 'em carved on rocks all over Yorkshire. Dad told me about 'em."

"What does it mean?"

"Man and woman. Sun and moon. So they say—no one really knows."

"The moon … ?" Lizzy was unexpectedly seized by an irresistible urge to leave. "Come on! Let's get out of here!"

They went back through the cleft in the rock.

"You were right. That was spooky!" Josh sighed with relief, and turned to follow their tracks back to the horses.

Lizzy grabbed him by the arm. "Stop!" she insisted. "That wasn't it. There's somewhere else I've got to go!"

Josh glanced at her anxiously. A strange, wild look had come over her. He was afraid.

Lizzy set off quickly through the bracken, and Josh struggled to keep up. His heart was thumping. The unearthly rock formations fed his fears, every few steps revealing another monstrous shape—a dog with wings, a vast oyster shell, a two-headed sphinx …

"Lizzy! Wait for me!" he shouted, but she carried on heedless. He kept falling in the snow, and the roots that tripped him seemed to clutch at his boots and refuse to let go.

He saw Lizzy arrive at the bottom of the highest of the rock formations—the top boulder was as flat as a table. The rocks were skiddy with snow but she clambered up without difficulty. Josh stumbled after her.

"Are you sure this is a good idea, Lizzy?"

He reached the top, panting. The rocks were perched on the edge of a cliff, and he could see for miles, right across to where the Yorkshire Dales rose out of the wide Swale valley, shrouded in snow. Dense woodland ran down the escarpment below them.

Lizzy pointed and whispered, " … Shalimar!"

Below the woods the ice-clad dome of the house glinted eerily in the full moonlight. As Lizzy gazed at it, she went still, her eyes fixed and glazed.

Josh looked at her in alarm. She walked towards to the edge of the cliff. He had a good head for heights, but even he felt vertigo.

"Careful, Lizzy!"

"Look! … "

Josh peered over the edge nervously as she pointed to the boulder-strewn slope directly below them.

" … That's where they found Aunt Penelope's body when she jumped off here!"

Josh almost tripped over in his haste to retreat. "You're m … m … making that up!" he stammered, backing away from her. The moon bathed her pale face in its hypnotic light.

"No, I'm not," Lizzy said. "Have you ever heard anything about the full-moon curse on my family?"

Josh shuffled uneasily. "Yeah, well, there's talk around the estate. You know … no one talks about it in front of you Abercrombies, mind."

"What do people say?"

"It's to do with all the fatal accidents at the full moon. Even your … " Josh's voice trailed off.

"Even my mum?"

Josh nodded quickly. He really didn't want to upset her.

Lizzy went silent for a moment. "What do they say has caused this curse, then?" she said eventually.

"The rumour is that it all started with something to do with your Uncle George. To do with India … "

"Lizzy!" A voice called from behind them. They both jumped out of their skins, turning …

"Uncle P … P … Peregrine!" Lizzy said. "What are you doing here?"

"Same as you, Lizzy," His voice was quiet and calm. "Looking for answers and finding only questions," he said, and disappeared into the night.

14

KNOWLESBY, TWO DAYS LATER

"ONE POUND NINETY."

Mrs Wu, the owner of The Plaice Place, looked at Lizzy and Josh without blinking. They scrambled in their pockets and counted out the amount they each needed to pay.

"And some scraps, please," Lizzy said, just as Mrs Wu was about to start wrapping their chips. She scooped up some scraps of fried batter and sprinkled them on top of the chip packets, while the people in the queue behind them tutted with impatience.

"Thanks!"

They walked out into the marketplace.

The thaw had turned the heavy Christmas snow on the pavements into a mixture of slush and grey-brown lumps left behind by the snow-ploughs. The sun shone down from a clear blue sky onto the centre of Knowlesby, and the old redbrick buildings that surrounded the marketplace glowed warmly in the early afternoon light.

They sat down on a bench near the market clock to eat. As it was two days after Christmas the town was heaving with shoppers looking for bargains. Pensioners wheeled their shopping bags awkwardly through the slush, and young mums wearing tight jeans and high-heeled boots headed towards the shops with complaining kids in tow.

"Mmmm! Delicious!" Josh said as he gobbled down his chips.

"They stick to your ribs!" Lizzy agreed, and he looked at her, puzzled.

"What do you mean?"

"Don't you know? It's an old Yorkshire way of saying 'they fill you up'."

"Never 'eard it."

"My mum told me it. When she first moved up here she bought a book of Yorkshire sayings. She used them all the time."

"Wasn't she from Yorkshire?"

"No, she was brought up in Africa."

"Wow!" Josh said, and they continued eating in silence.

Lizzy and Josh had taken the bus to Knowlesby together that morning. It was the first time they had seen each other since their adventure on the moors. After Peregrine had left the two of them had walked the horses down in silence.

"It were right spooky when your uncle appeared, wasn't it?" Josh said as he finished the last chip.

"Yeah, well he's like that … He's a Sufi. He meditates a lot. My mum always said that he knows stuff that no one else has even thought about."

"Mebbe you should ask him about the curse?"

"He's not the sort of person you can ask. You heard him. 'Looking for answers and finding only questions.'"

They scrumpled up the empty chip papers and threw them in the waste bin by the bus stop. As they walked aimlessly down the streets behind the market square, they went over everything they knew about the curse over and over again.

"I've got to find out what it's all about, Josh," Lizzy said finally, looking round her. They'd been so engrossed that they'd ended up in a bit of Knowlesby where she'd never been before.

And who should she see coming out of BinEndz, the tatty off-licence at the other side of the road, but Uncle William? He glanced around furtively, as if he didn't want to be seen, and Lizzy instinctively turned away to avoid being recognised. She nudged Josh. When she looked back, a wiry old lady had joined Uncle William.

A man came running out of the shop after her waving a bit of paper. "I'm sorry, I forgot to say that you haven't settled your account this month, Mrs Corker."

Mrs Corker? thought Lizzy with a start. *Wasn't that the name of ... ?*

"Mabel, please!" The old lady insisted, smiling at the manager. "You know me well enough ... " She passed the bill to Uncle William without looking at it.

"Mabel Corker!" Lizzy whispered to Josh. "That's Dad's old nanny! What's she doing here ... ?"

Uncle William reached into his pocket, pulling out a wad of notes as they followed the manager back into the shop.

"I haven't time to explain," Lizzy said under her breath, "but we've got to follow them!" Josh nodded his agreement. They hid in a shop doorway, and watched as Uncle William and the old lady came back out of the off-licence a minute later. As they headed up a leafy road with large houses set back in neat gardens, Lizzy and Josh followed at a safe distance. Uncle William and Mabel disappeared into an entrance driveway, and Lizzy and Josh arrived just in time to see them close the front door of a large brick building behind them. A sign by the entrance read 'Greenlawns Retirement Home'.

"What do we do next?" Josh asked.

"Keep following," Lizzy said. Bold as brass, she walked up the drive towards the door and Josh followed.

They entered—the deserted hallway smelt of disinfectant and cabbage. Edging cautiously along a corridor, they turned a corner, passing the open door of a common room where two old men were asleep in wheelchairs in front of a blaring television. Too late, Lizzy spotted Uncle William lumbering towards them carrying a thin briefcase.

He stopped dead when he saw them.

"Hello, Uncle William!" Lizzy said.

"What the hell are you two doing here?" he rasped.

"We ... we ... saw you with Mabel Corker!" Lizzy blurted out, backing away from him.

Uncle William was incandescent with rage, and looked at her with such intense loathing that her blood froze.

"I don't know what you're up to," he said, his face close to hers, pinning her to the wall. "But if you mention this to your father or anyone else, I'll make life very, very difficult for you!"

Lizzy was stunned into silence. Uncle William was usually so polite and ineffectual, but now she felt horribly threatened.

"I could throw you both out of Maya Lodge at the drop of a hat ... Do I make myself clear?"

"Y ... y ... yes," she nodded, petrified. "C ... c ... ompletely clear."

"And you!" Uncle William turned on Josh. "You're the Giddons boy, aren't you?" Josh nodded dumbly. "Your family will be out on their ear if you so much as breathe a word of this! Got that?"

"Y ... y ... yeah!" he stammered.

With a final, fierce glare Uncle William turned and strode down the corridor towards the front door. They were both shaking from the ferocity of his onslaught.

"Mabel was their nanny," Lizzy said eventually. "Uncle William told Dad he didn't remember her. But I knew he was lying … " She looked at Josh intently. "This is just too weird … !"

15

MABEL CORKER

HALF-AN-HOUR LATER, Mabel Corker opened the door and blinked at Josh and Lizzy through bleary eyes. The television was switched on in her room, and she looked as if she must have fallen asleep in front of it.

"What is it?"

"We've come from Mr Abercrombie," Lizzy explained. "He told us to give you these flowers. A late Christmas present, he said. He forgot them earlier."

"Well, that's a first!" Mabel said in a husky smoker's voice. She glanced at the meagre bunch. "He's really pushed the boat out, hasn't he just?" she said as she took them. "That lot must have cost all of a fiver."

Six quid, to be precise, Lizzy thought. It was all they could afford, and she hoped it would be worth it.

"Well, you'd better come in and keep an old gal company for a minute. I don't get many visitors." Mabel opened the door for Lizzy and Josh, and they walked into her room.

The sun streamed in through the big bay window which overlooked the lawn at the back of the house. It was a comfortable room, large and well furnished. The remains of Mabel's lunch sat on a tray on the table, along with an empty glass. A half-finished bottle of sherry stood on a sideboard.

"Sit down, sit down!" Mabel pointed to the comfy chairs in front of a gas fire. She switched the television off, and started to arrange the flowers in a vase. There was a framed photograph of Uncle William and Aunt Lavinia on their wedding day just by her.

Lizzy noticed it, and Mabel saw the direction of her glance. She nodded. "That's the Abercrombies, all right; it was a big society wedding, so I'm told—you can be sure I wasn't invited." She laughed mirthlessly. "Still, it serves to keep Mr A on his toes when he visits." A look of smug satisfaction came over Mabel's fine-featured face as she sat down. "I suppose your parents work at Shalimar?" She scrutinised them closely, narrowing her eyes.

Lizzy and Josh had worked out their story while they were walking from the flower shop. They both started it at the same time and stopped, blushing. Lizzy started again.

"Mum helps in the kitchen, and our dad's a gardener. He sent us to give Mr Abercrombie a hand with some shopping."

"Did he, now?" Mabel lit a cigarette, and breathed the smoke out through her nose. It uncurled languorously in the shafts of sunlight, like a cat stretching. "You live on the estate, then?" she asked.

"Yes, in one of the lodges," Lizzy replied nervously. She hoped Mabel wasn't going to question them too closely, but luckily she was more interested in her own thoughts.

"Nice little houses, aren't they? I remember … " She seemed about to tell them something of her past but then clammed up.

"How do you know Mr Abercrombie?" Lizzy asked with feigned innocence. Mabel's eyes sharpened suspiciously.

"Never you mind!" she said, a hard edge to her voice. "And I think you'd best be going now." She stood up abruptly, and bustled Lizzy and Josh out of the door.

"What did you say your names were?" Mabel called out just as they were setting off down the corridor.

"Goodbye!" Lizzy shouted, pretending not to hear.

As she closed the door behind her, Mabel leant against it, a worried expression on her thin face.

As they walked back towards the centre of town, they decided that Uncle William must be secretly keeping Mabel Corker at the retirement home. But why he should do that, they had no idea.

"She's got Uncle William's wedding photograph and but she won't say who she is," Lizzy said. "Very odd … "

"She's being as secretive as 'e is … "

"And she said she had the wedding photo 'to keep him on his toes'," Lizzy mused. "What did she mean by that?"

"Dunno … "

"So why is Uncle William looking after her now?"

Lizzy wished she could ask her father, but after what Uncle William had said it was too risky. She knew it was only because of her uncle that they lived in Maya Lodge rent-free, which made it possible for her father to pursue his scientific research.

They caught the bus to Nethermoorside and walked back in the fading light to Maya Lodge for tea. Looking at her much-loved home, it horrified Lizzy to think that Uncle William could take it away from them. Josh needed no reminder how serious the threat was—his family could lose everything that mattered too.

Lizzy frowned—Rose's Fiat was parked outside. When they went in they found her sitting at the dining table with her father—it was covered with books and sheets of paper.

Rose beamed broadly when she saw Lizzy. "Hi! Did you have a nice Christmas?"

"Yes, thanks," she replied automatically.

"Mine was nice, but dull," Rose said when Lizzy failed to enquire. "There wasn't any snow at my aunt's down south." She saw Josh who was standing in the door. "Hello, Joshua!"

" 'Ello." He looked shyly at his shoes.

Henry looked up. "Why don't you make our guests some tea, Lizzy?"

Rose jumped to her feet and offered to help.

As they stood together in the kitchen and Lizzy laid a tray, Rose told her that she had telephoned shortly after she'd left for Knowlesby. Henry and she had started chatting about poetry and he'd invited her to come and look at the work he was doing on translating Shakespeare's sonnets into modern English—and to see Lizzy, of course.

"It's marvellous what he's doing, Lizzy … " She blushed as she added, " … He said I was unusually knowledgeable."

Lizzy grimaced. Everything about Rose was becoming far too usual for her taste.

After they'd had tea, Josh left to walk home and Lizzy's father asked Rose if she'd like to read some more of his sonnet translations.

"I'd very much like to," Rose got to her feet, "but I'm afraid I've got to go."

"Another time, perhaps?"

"I'd love that. Goodbye—and congratulations!"

Henry looked momentarily baffled.

"On your sonnet project. I think it's a brave and exciting thing you're doing."

Brave and exciting? Those were not words she usually associated with her father, Lizzy thought, as he saw Rose to the door.

16

WILLIAM HAS A PLAN

A FEW EVENINGS LATER William Abercrombie sat in his study nervously drumming his fingers on the desk. He was a worried man. He was gambling on Henry's concerns about Lizzy—surely his brother couldn't turn down what he was going to propose?

When William had told Lavinia his plan, she'd been horrified at what it would cost, but he'd won her round in the end. Most of the time he gave into his wife, but on this occasion she'd given in to him—Lavinia had never seen him so serious and decisive.

William smiled to himself cynically. Of course the only thing he hadn't told her was the real reason why he had to do it. If she knew that …

There was a knock at the door.

William forced himself to concentrate on what he was going to say to Henry.

"Come in," he said, struggling out of his chair. Henry opened the door and they shook hands. "Hello, Henry! Scotch?"

"Please. This is all very mysterious, William," Henry said as his brother handed him a glass. "You have a proposal which may well interest me, you said?"

"Yes." William fingered his collar and swallowed. "I've been thinking," he said. "You know our conversation on Christmas Day?"

"Yes? ... "

"It seems to me that the best thing for Lizzy would be a change of scenery ... get her away from Shalimar and everything."

"Yes? ... "

"Well, what do you think about the idea of sending her to board at Laythorpe College? They have excellent facilities there."

Henry frowned. "I'm sure they do, William, but you know very well I can't afford it ... "

"I'll pay."

"What?" Henry looked at his brother in astonishment. He wasn't normally known for his generosity.

"I'll be delighted to pay for her. She is my niece, after all ... "

"Yes, but ... " Henry struggled with the idea of William being a caring uncle. He'd shown no sign of it before. "And Lavinia's happy about this?" Lavinia's meanness was legendary. She docked the staff's wages if they so much as broke a cup.

"It was her idea." William had decided it was essential to say that, even though he thought it sounded implausible. He didn't want Lizzy putting two and two together. He waited nervously for Henry's reaction.

"Lavinia's idea?" He was astounded.

"Yes. I told her about our little chat, and she was very concerned for Lizzy, particularly after the way she behaved. She thinks she needs a complete change."

"That's something we all can agree on, but Laythorpe College?" He shook his head in disbelief. He and Alice had long been concerned that Lizzy's education was suffering at the local schools, and the College had one of the best academic records in the country ...

"And there's the riding, of course ... "

"Look, it's a fantastic offer, William, and I can't tell you how touched I am. But are you absolutely sure you want to do this? ... "

"I'm on the College Board of Governors, as you know, Henry," he said. "I can get a very good deal." This was untrue, but William thought it might help Henry to accept the idea. "And I've established that she can start next term—no problem with changing schools and all that kerfuffle."

"Really?" said Henry dubiously.

"Absolutely. They get pupils from all over the world, so they're used to things happening at a moment's notice."

Henry shook his head again. "I'm stunned, William, absolutely stunned. I can't thank you enough."

"Don't mention it. That's what families are for, Henry." He looked relieved. "So that's agreed then?"

"Yes, of course ... I'll have to ask Lizzy, naturally, but I just need to say the word 'horse' ... "

"And she jumps! ... " William chuckled at his own joke.

"Exactly." Henry reflected for a moment. "You've told the Sams about this, I suppose?"

William went pale. *The Sams!* he thought. *I've forgotten all about the Sams!*

Lavinia and William told them over dinner. The Sams were appalled.

"You must be kidding!" said Samantha, downing her knife and fork and turning pink with indignation.

"She doesn't have a clue about how to behave!" Samuel said. "She'll embarrass us! Look at her friends—"

"If she's got any," chipped in Samantha.

"Joshua Giddons. I mean, I ask you … Joshua! His father's the groom."

"And not very good at that, either," Samantha said. "Stetson's saddle hadn't been cleaned properly when I rode him on Boxing Day. And he was tired and out of condition."

"But my darlings!" Lavinia said. "We're not saying that you'll have to spend all your time with Lizzy. She's the year behind you, and she'll soon make friends of her own."

The Sams snorted in unison. "Her?" said Samuel. "She'll be lucky if anyone even talks to her!"

"Yes," Samantha agreed. "They're all very sophisticated at school. Lizzy's just a—"

"Peasant!" Samuel finished. "She's got a Yorkshire accent!"

"Which she tries to hide—"

"Naturally!"

"And then she'll want to come to all the parties we go to!" Samantha continued.

"If anyone invites her."

"Which they won't!"

William was seething with impatience. "Look, it's been decided, and that's an end to it."

"Who decided?" Samantha challenged. "You didn't ask us!"

"I decided," William said. "Now like it or lump it!"

The Sams looked at him amazed. Their father had become much more forceful since Christmas.

Lavinia adopted a more diplomatic approach. "It's because we think it's best for Lizzy, darlings!"

"And what about us? You never think what's best for us!"

"Yes," Samuel agreed. "All of a sudden it's Lizzy this and Lizzy that. We are your children, remember!"

"And she's just a cousin. A poor cousin."

The Sams sniggered in unison.

"Why don't you adopt her?" Samuel said. "Uncle Henry doesn't want her … "

"Who can blame him?"

"She can live here and move into the best bedroom—"

"She's always liked it—"

"And you can cut us out of your will. Leave us starving—"

"In the gutter—"

"Guttersnipes!"

"Just like her!" finished Samantha.

William struggled to keep his temper. He never ceased to be amazed at the Sams' ability to talk as if they had rehearsed everything they were going to say to perfection before saying it. He thumped the table. That got their attention.

"Lizzy goes to Laythorpe," he glared at the Sams. "And if I hear another word out of you two, I'll send you to Knowlesby Grammar."

The Sams instantly went silent.

"You'll be starting next term, then?" asked Josh. He was sitting with Lizzy in their favourite hiding place above the stables. It had used to be a room for storing hay, but now it contained mainly broken garden tools and the odd dead spider.

"Yes!" Lizzy said. She hadn't yet got over the shock of what her father had told her the previous day. "There's an enormous indoor school for the horses, jumps outside, a swimming pool and you can learn tennis and everything. And then they make you go to Oxford or Cambridge." She wasn't sure about the last bit, but she thought she'd read it in the school's prospectus Uncle William had given them. "And the bedrooms have all got kettles! It's better than home!"

"Bedrooms? You'll be boarding?" Josh tried to look pleased as he tickled Benjy under the chin.

"Yeah, of course! It's a boarding school! Duh!" Lizzy paused, suddenly noticing that Josh wasn't as enthusiastic as she was about her news. "But they let you come home for some weekends during the terms, and then there's the holidays … "

"Yeah, well it sounds brilliant, Lizzy. And Mr Abercrombie's paying for it all?"

"Dad's paying for the uniforms and extras, of course," Lizzy said. She didn't want to sound like she was a charity case. "The riding is all included, though." She could see the video of the riding facilities in her mind's eye. "They let you keep horses there, too. You know, like the Sams. But Dad says I'll have to use the school's horses. It's cheaper."

"So whose idea was it to send you to Laythorpe?"

"Aunt Lavinia's, apparently. She thought of it at Christmas." Lizzy blushed at the recollection of her outburst that day. Thankfully her father hadn't mentioned it since.

Josh leant back in the broken chair he was sitting on. "No more Susan Birkinshaw, then?"

"That's a relief."

" … And no more school bus with Delice Tasker showing off?"

"I never thought she had much to show off about anyway."

"That's true … " Josh grinned. "And no more Rose Franklin?"

"Thank God! She meddles in everything. Dad even rang her up to ask her what she thought of me going away to school. Fortunately she said it was a brilliant idea."

There was a silence.

Josh reflected that it was as if Lizzy had already moved on to another world from which he was for ever excluded.

On the last day of the school holidays Lizzy went to visit the place where her mother had died, to say goodbye.

It was a cold, cloudy day, and a gentle drizzle was falling as she walked across the Shalimar Park. When she got to the Brahmin Bridge, instead of crossing it she took a path that led down to the Snake Pool, and followed it further through the Indian Garden. Winter had turned the vibrant green plants into sorry, limp lettuces. Soon she came to the cedars, their branches spread out horizontally like dancers in a majestic ballet.

She felt her chest tightening. She remembered leading Fire down here on the fateful morning and saw the tree where she had tethered him. Taking a deep breath she rounded the enormous trunk—and gave a cry of shock.

"Don't be afraid, Lizzy!" Peregrine said. He was sitting cross-legged on the grass with his back to her and raised his right hand as if commanding the world to be still.

"How … how did you know it was me?" Lizzy stammered.

"Who else could it be?" He stood up with a slow, fluid movement that appeared almost effortless. He was wearing a pair of green corduroy trousers and a strange yellow tunic that seemed to button up both sides. He looked at her with his ethereal grey eyes. "Is it the first time you've been back here?"

"I came once before. A few weeks ago."

"Would you like me to leave?" he asked.

Lizzy thought of how he used to frighten her, and how he had appeared so mysteriously on the moors. But there was something reassuring in his presence now, so calm and undemanding.

"I'd like you to stay. Please." Lizzy said. She looked around her—Peregrine had been sitting just where she had found her mother. Her mind flashed back to the image of her lying dead on the grass, her blood oozing into the patchy snow.

"Your mother particularly loved this spot," Peregrine said. "The cedars, and of course the weeping hornbeam … " He pointed to a tree nearby, trailing its long tendrils like rats' tails. Even without their leaves, they formed a curtain through which it was difficult to see. "It's a mutant—did you know that?"

"What does that mean?"

"Come." He parted the curtain, and led her under the canopy of the tree. It was like being inside an exquisite marquee, the trailing sprigs swaying quietly in the breeze. "Look at these strange twists in the branches like enormous old ropes, and the way they head off in one direction and then seem to change their minds, and then change them again. That's not what weeping hornbeams are usually like. This tree is a one-off, a unique specimen, there's no other one like it anywhere. Your mother knew that."

Peregrine looked directly at Lizzy. "They think a meteorite landed nearby when it was just a seed. Changed its genes. Irrevocably." He gestured towards the sky. "A bolt from the blue! Something totally unexpected happens and life is utterly different. That's what Alice loved so much about this tree. The wild, improbable beauty of it."

There was something almost hypnotic in the way Peregrine spoke. It was as if suddenly Lizzy were looking at the world through different eyes; eyes more intense, more aware.

He held back the branches and they walked under the cedar.

Lizzy looked at the spot where her mother had died. "You don't think her death was an accident either, do you?" she asked Peregrine softly.

Peregrine put his hand on her shoulder for a moment. "Was that meteor an accident? … "

Lizzy shuddered, and then he turned and walked away.

17

LAYTHORPE COLLEGE

"BREATHE IN SLOWLY FROM the bottom of your stomach and feel your lungs filling with air right up to your throat. Hold the breath for a moment, then release it slowly … "

Lizzy heard her mother's voice in her head as she did her early morning yoga exercises in the Laythorpe College gym. There was usually no one else around, but this morning she could hear the clatter of metal from the weight-training room. She didn't let the noise put her off—she needed the release of tension that her yoga gave her.

The first few weeks at her new school had been very difficult. Right from the start the Sams had set about undermining her with a vengeance, spreading rumours that Lizzy was their 'poor relation'. Most of the pupils at the College were from wealthy backgrounds, many from abroad, and it was if they were members of an exclusive club and couldn't understand how Lizzy had been allowed to join.

As a result, she had kept herself pretty much to herself. The three other girls she shared her bedroom with in Wykeham House already had their own friends and didn't seem in a hurry to add Lizzy to the list. And while compared to Knowlesby Grammar the teaching and the facilities were fantastic, it meant that she'd had to work very hard to catch up with the others in her classes.

Nearly all the rest of her spare time was spent in the equestrian centre—there at least she felt welcome. The assistant head riding teacher was Alison Studley, a no-nonsense local girl who took Lizzy under her wing. She'd ridden quite a few of the College horses and was getting much better at jumping, although none of the horses were as bold as Stetson. She'd often seen Samantha riding him, and would have loved to have tried him out over the jumps in the indoor arena but her cousin wouldn't let her.

"You'll ruin him," she said to Lizzy when she'd asked. "He's not a novice ride, you know."

"And she isn't a novice rider," Alison said, jumping to Lizzy's defence. "She'll be better than you soon enough, I tell you … "

Samantha had simply smirked. Alison couldn't force her to let Lizzy ride Stetson, and she knew it.

"Brace your thigh muscles and tuck the bottom of your spine under … stretch the rest of your back upwards and raise your hands above your head … "

Lizzy could sense the presence of someone behind her in the gym, watching her doing her postures. She completed the movement before turning round to see who it was.

A handsome Indian boy about her age stood nearby, with a towel around his neck. He had thick, dark hair and dreamy brown eyes.

"Sorry," he said, "I didn't mean to disturb you."

"It's okay," said Lizzy. "You didn't."

She knew exactly who the boy was. All the pupils at the College did. Ravi Chandra was the son of the famous film director who was about to start shooting *The Lifeline*.

"Do you do yoga?" Lizzy asked.

"No, but I'm starting to do weights," he replied, smiling with a flash of white teeth. "I'm trying to build up these puny muscles … " He flexed his biceps theatrically, and Lizzy giggled. Ravi was known for being super-brainy and top of every class, but no one had ever seen him take any interest in sports.

Lizzy flexed her own biceps. They were more muscly than Ravi's, and they both burst out laughing.

"Yoga's becoming very fashionable in India, you know," Ravi told Lizzy. He had a slight American twang to his voice.

"But wasn't it invented there?" she asked, surprised.

"It was, yes, but that was in ancient times, and now-adays city people in India are mainly interested in modern things … "

"Like weight training … " said Lizzy.

"Yeah. There are gyms all over."

"So why's yoga fashionable?"

"Because it's become very popular in the US and UK. So in India it's now seen as the hot new thing."

"We're teaching you something you taught us?" Lizzy asked. "That seems a bit ridiculous … "

Ravi laughed. "That's one way of looking at it." He looked at Lizzy curiously. "Who taught you?"

"My mother."

"Is she a yoga teacher?"

"No, she wasn't. But she loved it … "

"Wasn't? … "

"She died. A couple of years ago."

"I'm sorry ... " Ravi said, and Lizzy noticed he didn't say it in the meaningless, automatic way most people did; nor did he assume a tone of exaggerated concern. She smiled at him.

"You should try it," she said. "You'd soon build up those muscles—and discover ones you never even knew that you had. And imagine how fashionable you'd become ... " she added mischievously. "You'd be fighting off the girls."

As she knew full well, Ravi was already fighting off the girls, at least those at Laythorpe College. Two of her roommates were amongst them, and they talked non-stop about how gorgeous he was and how glamorous his father must be. Samantha was desperate to become his friend too, Lizzy knew, and was forever finding ways to bump into him in the corridors.

Ravi never noticed any of them, much to their disappointment. Nor had he much time for any of the boys who had tried to befriend him. He spent every spare hour glued to his computer screen, not playing trivial games, but studying no one knew what.

Ravi looked at Lizzy with interest. "Do you think you could teach me?"

"There's no reason why I couldn't show you the basics," Lizzy replied. "Here, let's try this one." She stood with her legs spread wide apart and slowly folded forwards from the waist, her arms stretched out in front of her.

"What, right now?" Ravi said dubiously.

"There's no time like the present" Lizzy's head was down by her feet. She unfolded again.

She spent the next ten minutes running Ravi through a few routines including the 'Sun Salutation'. Lizzy was surprised how stiff and uncoordinated he was, as if he existed only in his head and hardly knew that he had a body. But his powers of concentration were amazing—he might not get the positions right, but she only had to show him each sequence once for him to know it by heart.

"That's it for today," she said finally. "We'll go through them again tomorrow, and then I'll show you some more complicated positions."

Ravi smiled. "So you don't think it's ridiculous, then?"

"What?" said Lizzy, puzzled.

"You teaching me, an Indian, how to do yoga?"

Lizzy shrugged. "No, but it's ridiculous that you're such a geriatric. You can hardly touch your knees, never mind your toes. But the Abercrombie School of Yoga will sort you out."

Ravi laughed. "Is Abercrombie your name?"

She nodded. "But now that I am now officially your guru, you may call me Lizzy."

"I'm Ravi … "

"I know … "

They walked out of the gym together. It was a grim January day, and the rain was being driven by the gusts of wind so that even under the covered walkway leading back to the houses they had keep to one side of the path to avoid getting wet.

They were approaching the entrance to Wykeham House when Pippi Weiss, a blonde American girl who was one of Lizzy's roommates, caught sight of them as she was coming out of the door.

She stopped immediately and greeted Lizzy warmly.

"Hi, Lizzy, how was your yoga? I'm like so impressed that you do it every day." Lizzy responded with a fleeting smile— all the girls in her bedroom knew she practised yoga, but they hadn't shown the slightest interest before. Pippi looked expectantly at Lizzy, and her eyes flicked for a moment to Ravi. "Oh, sorry!" Lizzy said, remembering her manners. "This is Ravi."

"Hi! I'm Pippi! I room with Lizzy." She gave him a dazzling smile. "Are you kinda like from India or something?"

Lizzy thought this was an odd question, considering how much time Pippi and Daphne Newman spent in their bedroom dissecting every detail they knew of Ravi's life.

Ravi muttered something about having just moved back to Mumbai from California.

"Like I would just so love to go to India," Pippi continued. "You know, like Angkor Wat by moonlight must be like totally awesome."

"Angkor Wat is in Cambodia," Ravi said.

"Sure, yeah, whatever," Pippi continued blithely. "My dad says he may like take us there at Easter. He's in real estate. What does your father do?"

Ravi mumbled something that sounded like 'astronaut'.

Pippi carried on regardless. "Isn't that just great? I wanna get into movies myself. Mom keeps putting me up for auditions, but I'm like so busy with my modelling I just don't have the time." She preened herself as if she were in front of a camera.

Ravi turned suddenly to Lizzy. "Listen, I've got to go, Lizzy. See you later." Then he hurried away towards Ascham House.

"Isn't he like totally hot?" said Pippi. "And did you like see that look he gave me?"

Like he couldn't wait to get away, thought Lizzy. She suddenly felt rather sorry for Ravi. Just because his father was famous everyone wanted a piece of him.

18

WORD GETS AROUND

WHEN SHE SPOTTED HIM later in their English class Ravi grinned, and at the end hobbled over to her.

"I'm in agony, Lizzy," he groaned, half-seriously. "I didn't know yoga was a form of torture."

"Don't worry—it can only get better."

"Talking of torture, is that Pippi really your room-mate?"

Lizzy nodded. "Like, she may sound like she's like totally stupid," she said, "but like I quite like her. Like."

Ravi burst out laughing at Lizzy's impersonation, and she noticed that she was attracting lots of envious glances from the other pupils as they filed past them out of the classroom.

"Is this the first time you've been away from home?" Ravi asked.

Lizzy nodded.

"Are you missing it?"

Lizzy thought for a moment. "Not really. Since my mum died it hasn't really seemed like home anyway."

"I've been boarding at one school or another since I was six," Ravi said. "And we've moved so often with my Dad's job that I haven't really ever had a home to miss. That's why we've moved back to Mumbai. Dad says that he's determined to spend at least half the year there."

"Have you got any brothers or sisters?"

Ravi shook his head.

"Me neither," said Lizzy.

"But I've got lots of cousins back in Mumbai."

The only cousins I have are the Sams, Lizzy reflected. *And a fat lot of use they are.*

They walked together past the front of the main school building, a Victorian manor house built in the Tudor style with weathered bricks and vast leaded windows. The lights in the great oak-panelled hall shone into the darkness, and their shadows stretched across the immaculate lawns.

"I've got to go," Lizzy said as they approached Wykeham House, "But I'll see you early tomorrow for yoga."

"*Namaste*, Lizzy," Ravi said, putting his hands together and bowing.

"What does that mean?" Lizzy asked.

"'I bow to you.'"

"I haven't heard that before."

"So the student becomes the teacher," Ravi said with a grin as he walked away.

When she walked into Wykeham House she found Samantha waiting for her, smiling as pleasantly as she could manage.

"Cuz, I've been looking for you absolutely every-where!" she cooed. "I hear you've made friends with Ravi Chandra … "

Crikey! News travels fast round here! Lizzy thought. She was hardly even aware that she was friends with him herself.

"I've been wanting to invite him for a weekend at Shalimar—you know, him being Indian and all that. It might make him feel at home."

"Well, invite him then," said Lizzy. She didn't see what it had to do with her. "The worst he can do is say no."

"I thought it might be better coming from you," Samantha said in her silkiest voice. "Seeing as how you're friends now."

"Shalimar is your house, not mine," Lizzy said. "I can't ask him to someone else's home."

Samantha pouted petulantly. "But you know how welcome you always are to come to Shalimar, cuz. It's nearly your house, too."

She's changed her tune, Lizzy thought as Samantha flounced out. Usually the Sams were about as welcoming as a deep freeze. It annoyed her that suddenly, just because she had struck up a bit of a friendship with Ravi, people wanted to use her as a way of getting to him.

She told Ravi what had happened with Samantha when they met up for yoga next morning.

"Has it always been like this?" she asked.

"No, not at all. I mean Dad's made some pretty famous films, but it's not as if most people are really interested in a director, and certainly not his son. But since he started working on *The Lifeline* it's been crazy … "

" … The book's been so successful that everyone's dying to see the film."

"Yeah. Shankar's hardly had a moment's peace."

Lizzy's eyes opened wide in disbelief. "You know Shankar Pujari?" she blurted out. The author of *The Lifeline* was unbelievably famous.

99

"See?" Ravi sighed. "Even you can't help being impressed."

They laughed, and Lizzy could sense Ravi's relief that he had someone to talk to in a normal way.

They went through the exercises that she had shown him the day before, and then she taught him some new ones. They were both so absorbed in what they were doing they could think of nothing else.

When they had finished, they sat on a gym bench to recover. Lizzy told him a bit about Uncle George and Shalimar. Ravi was intrigued.

"I'd love to see it someday, Lizzy," he said. "But only if you invite me … " he added with a shy smile.

When Lizzy went back to their room later, Emi Tamashige lifted her head from her book long enough to tell her that Aunt Lavinia had telephoned, and had asked Lizzy to call back. She was puzzled—Lizzy couldn't remember ever being called by her aunt before.

"Darling," Aunt Lavinia gushed when Lizzy rang back, "I'm so glad you phoned. I just wanted to tell you that if you want to ask any friends back for the coming weekend exeat to visit Shalimar, they'd be very welcome to stay."

Samantha's put her up to this! Lizzy thought.

"And you can stay here with him, too, of course … "

Him! So it was clear who she had in mind …

"You know our house is your house, too, Lizzy."

First Samantha and now Aunt Lavinia! But at least she wasn't doing it just because of Ravi—she seemed to have changed her attitude to Lizzy ever since she had had the idea to send her to Laythorpe …

Another thought occurred to her.

"If I stay, can I sleep in the guest room with the four poster and the murals?" she asked. It was a room Lizzy had always loved, but Aunt Lavinia had never allowed her to sleep in it. There was a silence at the other end of the telephone for a moment while her aunt digested this request.

"I'm not sure about that." Lavinia was very particular about who slept in the main guest room.

"I was thinking, if I had that room, maybe I could ask Ravi Chandra," Lizzy said casually. "He's a particular friend of mine."

"Ah. Well, I suppose you can have it, if you want," her aunt conceded.

"Thanks, Auntie," Lizzy said smiling to herself. Knowing celebrities certainly had its uses ...

19

TWO BOYS

"COME ON, RAVI!"

Exasperated, Lizzy shouted down from the top of the waterfall above the pool in Eden Beck. Ravi couldn't hear because of the sound of the rushing water, and in any case he was too busy puffing and panting to reply.

Lizzy wasn't impressed with his performance today. What could you say about someone who had never worn wellies? He'd looked at them suspiciously as if they were going to eat his feet, and had only reluctantly taken off his immaculate white trainers when Lizzy had told him they would get filthy and wet. Then he'd lagged behind all the way up Shrike's Wood and, worst of all, he'd refused to squeeze under the fallen tree trunk as she usually did, so she'd had to find a way round through the wet tangle of rhododendrons.

Now Ravi was peering up at her cluelessly from beside the pool.

"Come on, for Heaven's sake!"

After he caught up she led the way along the drove road to Grimstone Scar. Lizzy told him more about Uncle George, and how the night he vanished he had gone to London to have dinner with an old friend from India at his club and had never been seen again.

"But the friend was found dead in the Turkish baths where he and Uncle George had been talking," Lizzy added. "He'd died of a heart attack in the night."

"Who was the friend?"

"No one knew. They could tell he'd been in India because of his uniform and things, but no more than that … "

"How strange!" Ravi said. "Where did George live in India when he was there?"

"Ask my dad. I think he knows some of that family history stuff."

They hadn't yet had a chance to visit Henry, who was out at work until lunchtime.

When they had arrived that morning Lizzy had rushed upstairs to put her case in the guest bedroom. Dominating it was a magnificent four-poster bed made out of carved wood. Four pillars shaped like lances with gold-painted blades at the top supported a wooden dome, the same shape and shade of green as the dome of Shalimar. The whole bed was draped in canary-yellow silk hand-painted with running cheetahs, prowling tigers and leaping deer.

The walls of the bedroom were covered from floor to ceiling with a mural of a vast Indian landscape, craggy mountains topped with temples, streams rushing down through densely forested gorges, loin-clothed pilgrims walking barefoot up steep paths, and distant cities gleaming in the valleys beyond.

Tindy Postlethwaite had shown Ravi the Bengal Room where he was staying, and he and Lizzy met on the landing. She showed him her room and he whistled in wonder.

"Does India still look like these murals?" Lizzy asked.

Ravi smiled. "Less and less, but scenes like these still exist in places." He looked around him. "This is amazing!" But then he was amazed by the whole house—he'd never seen anything like it in his life.

The Sams had gone off shopping with Aunt Lavinia in Knowlesby. Lizzy insisted that she and Ravi went straight away to the Giddons' cottage to find Josh, but he wasn't at home, and his father told her he was exercising one of the horses on the moor. Lizzy wanted to show off everything and everyone to Ravi, and she decided they should go to Grimstone Scar. Maybe they'd bump into Josh up there, she'd thought hopefully …

Ravi was struck by the beauty of the view when they got to the Scar, although it was a blustery day, and grey clouds hung heavily over the landscape obscuring the distant hills. Occasional raindrops spotted the waxed jackets they had borrowed from the cloakroom at Shalimar, whose green dome Lizzy pointed out through the bare trees down below, all the while keeping a lookout for Josh. Eventually his slight figure appeared on horseback trotting along the drove road towards the Scar, with Benjy scampering behind. She waved her hands and shouted; when Josh saw her, he waved back, and put his horse into canter.

"That's him! My friend, Josh." She set off at a run down from the Scar to the drove road, Ravi puffing along behind through the heather.

"Now then, Lizzy!" said Josh, a broad smile cracking his pale face as he stopped the horse and slid out of the saddle. There was a moment's awkwardness between the two of them—they were both far too shy to hug each other, and shaking hands would have been ridiculous. Lizzy leant down to pat Benjy whose tail was wagging madly.

Josh thought to himself how much more self-assured Lizzy looked, and prettier, too. Her glossy dark hair caught the breeze, and she looked more grown-up somehow.

Lizzy stood straight again, and he quickly looked away.

"You're riding Fire!" Lizzy said, to break the silence.

"Yeah. 'E's champion. Your aunt 'ardly ever takes him out, and me Dad asked 'er if it were all right if I exercised him."

"Wow, that's nice ... " Lizzy said. She liked riding at school, but it was nothing like galloping across the moors. That was something else.

Ravi came up to where they were standing, panting from his exertions and eyeing Fire nervously.

"This is Ravi," Lizzy told Josh. "My friend from school." She'd texted Josh about him a couple of times. He gave Ravi an appraising look.

"Now then," he said, with a curt nod.

Ravi stepped forwards and held out his hand. "You must be Josh. Lizzy's told me so much about you!" he said effusively.

"'As she now?" Josh shook Ravi's hand awkwardly. He'd grown a couple of inches since she'd last seen him, Lizzy noticed, and his fine, freckled features framed by his straw-blond hair were becoming very handsome.

"It's wonderful up here, isn't it?" Ravi continued. There was something about this taciturn stranger that made him nervous. "The views, and the way the light changes ... " He petered out.

Josh didn't reply.

"Ravi's dad makes films," Lizzy said, by way of explanation.

There was a gust of wind, and Fire stamped impatiently. Ravi jumped back like a startled rabbit, and nearly tumbled over in the heather.

"And he doesn't like horses," Lizzy added.

"I can see that. I'd best be getting out of 'is way, then." Josh jumped back into the saddle. "See you, Lizzy," he said. "Ravi," he added with a nod in his direction, and then cantered off with a clatter of hooves.

"We'll be round later … " Lizzy called after him.

Lizzy had the distinct impression that Josh didn't like Ravi, although she couldn't imagine why.

She felt a bit sorry for Ravi, who was looking bedraggled and ill-at-ease in his wellies as he watched the retreating back of Josh.

"C'mon, let's go down and see my dad. He should be back home by now. We're having lunch with him."

20

RAVI AND HENRY

H ENRY WAS PLEASED TO SEE Lizzy looking so well and full of life, and quickly warmed to Ravi, who was very well-mannered and seemed intelligent—both qualities that he admired. Lizzy noticed that the Lodge dining table was laid for four people, and looked at her father enquiringly.

"I've invited Rose … She really wants to see you, and I knew you'd like to see her, too."

Rose? Huh! I'd forgotten all about her … Lizzy thought.

While they were waiting for her to come, Henry asked Ravi what he thought of Shalimar and inevitably the conversation got around to Uncle George. Ravi asked where he had lived in India.

"Family history isn't really my bag," Henry said. "Although I know some of the Abercrombies have done bits and bobs over the years. But I'm pretty sure that George lived in a city called Junagadh. There's a very fine inlaid ivory and mother-of-pearl writing desk in the living room that belonged to George. Lavinia had it valued recently, and they said that the workmanship was typical of the city."

"Oh, yeah, I've heard about Junagadh," Ravi said. "It's supposed to be an amazing place. In fact all the surrounding

109

Saurashtra peninsula is full of ancient legends. The book Dad's filming is set there."

"Really?" Lizzy said. "*The Lifeline*?"

"Yeah. Shankar based his plot on some sacred Indian stories which are supposed to have happened in Saurashtra."

"Did you say '*The Lifeline*'?" Henry said. "That's the book you told me about, isn't it, Lizzy? With a heroine called Sita?"

"That's right!" Ravi said. "Sita and Ram, the two main characters are straight out of the *Ramayana*."

"Wow!" Lizzy said. "When were the books written?"

"Some say they date from as long ago as one thousand BC. They're older than the Old Testament."

"The many Gods of the East preceded the monolithic monotheism of the West," Henry said, almost to himself.

"And when you've only got one God, he can rule with an iron fist," Ravi said. "I've always thought the Indian system was more flexible."

"You could do with being more flexible, Ravi," Lizzy said. "You still can't touch your toes."

"Yeah. I don't know how I'm going to keep up yoga without you during the Easter holidays. In fact, I'll be joining my Dad on location in Gir forest at Easter— Junagadh is about twenty miles away, the other side of Girnar Mountain."

"Lizzy," her father said. "Get the atlas, would you?"

Lizzy jumped up and went to fetch the huge book from the bottom shelf.

"I gather from what you say that your father is in the film business, Ravi," her father said. "Has he made anything I might have seen?"

"Probably not, Dad," Lizzy answered for him, clearing a space on the dining table for the atlas. "You haven't been to the cinema since *The Sound of Music* came out."

"That's not true!" her father answered with a laugh, opening it. "Let's see now, Junagadh … " He leafed his way through the index

"Aren't you on the Internet, Mr Abercrombie?" Ravi asked. "Yes, of course," he answered. "But I prefer the old-fashioned way. You really get a sense of where you are with an atlas, and all the physical features of the landscape are so beautifully rendered. A map is like a work of art. Ah, here we go! Junagadh. Map thirty-seven, three c G 9." He turned the large pages slowly, and stopped at a map of the Indian subcontinent spread over two pages.

"It is beautiful," Ravi said. "But would you mind if I used your computer. Mr Abercrombie? I left my laptop back at Shalimar."

"Of course not!" Henry said. "Help yourself, Ravi—it's through there, in my study."

Ravi jumped to his feet and went out of the room.

Just as Henry was pointing to small peninsula in the north-west corner of the map and saying "There it is! Junagadh!" Ravi came back, reading aloud from a sheaf of papers.

"Junagadh … Muslim independent state in Saurashtra, Gujarat until 1948—that'll have been after Partition, obviously," Ravi added, handing Henry a map of the town and its immediate vicinity, a printout of the family tree of the ruling Nawabs, and a photograph of a walled fortress with a high mountain looming over it. "Population 185,590—although, knowing India, it'll be more by now. Asokan inscriptions, ancient fort, Jain Temple, etcetera, etcetera … When was your Uncle George in India?"

111

"Um … around 1850 or so, I think," Henry replied.

Who was ruling in 1853? … " He looked at Henry expectantly; he in turn stared at Ravi open-mouthed.

"Um, let me see," Henry said, bewildered. He leafed frenetically through the papers he had been given. Ravi's speediness was infectious. "Nawab Mahabatkhan II, if this is to be believed."

"And when was this Uncle George of yours in India?" said Ravi, tapping the toes of his right foot impatiently.

"Around that time, if I remember rightly … " Henry responded. He felt as if he were a lazy pupil faced with a tyrannical teacher.

"There you are then. The East India Company appointed someone—it doesn't say whom—as the first Resident to the State of Junagadh in 1853. He stayed until 1858 … "

"Sounds right!" added Henry. "George married Penelope in 1859—if I remember rightly."

" … Another Resident was appointed for a short while—then the position lapsed as it was decided to centralise the administration in Rajkot. So it looks like George was there from 1853 until 1858 during the reign of Nawab Mahabatkhan II."

"How did you manage to do all that so quickly?" Henry looked at Ravi in astonishment.

"I'll show you if you like," Ravi said, and the two of them retreated into Henry's study. Lizzy was quietly amused. She'd never seen her father so impressed.

Ravi may be hopeless on the moors, she thought, regretting her earlier impatience. *But he's great on the Web!"*

There was a loud knock on the front door, and before anyone answered, it opened.

"It's me!" Rose's voice called out. "Anyone home?"

21

TEATIME AT SHALIMAR

"So what was Uncle George actually doing in India?"
Lizzy asked Ravi later that afternoon as they stood on
the stairs at Shalimar looking at his portrait.

Ravi paused thoughtfully. "Have you learnt anything in
school about the British Empire, Lizzy?" he asked.

"The usual stuff," Lizzy said. "But I feel I've learnt a lot
about India just from living here—you know, the Surya
Temple, the Brahmin Bridge and all that. Plus my Mum
was really keen on India, obviously, with her yoga."

"Do you know how George made his fortune?" Ravi
asked,

"I am not sure he did—his wife Penelope was very rich
apparently."

Ravi laughed. "Anyway, plenty of you Brits did very well
out of India. They tell you that in school, don't they?"

"Sure. They say that they—we—exploited India and
were vicious and racist and tried to so-called civilise it."

"All perfectly true, of course. But then India has been
conquered and 'civilised' so many times in its history—
that's why it's so culturally rich."

"It's like what the Romans did to Britain," Lizzy said,
"and we prefer to forget that once we were the ones being

113

'civilised'. Like we forget that the French conquered us in 1066."

"No one likes to be reminded of the colonial yoke," Ravi said.

"I know. It's ridiculous really—the whole history of the world is about cultures rising and spreading. My mum told me that the English language has its roots in ancient Indian ... "

"Sanskrit," said Ravi.

"But I suppose the point is that we were in India in living memory—and did some pretty awful things, you know, like shooting all those innocent protesters with machine guns at Amritsar."

"Not your finest moment." Ravi murmured.

"But at least we did leave voluntarily in the end. You didn't have to kick us out."

"Yes. Partition and Independence in 1947." Ravi said. "It's what the Indians and Pakistanis wanted. In fact, lots of them would say that leaving was the only good thing the British ever accomplished."

"And you?" Lizzy asked. "What do you say?"

"Ravi! Lizzy!" Aunt Lavinia's strident voice called from the upstairs drawing room. "Tea is served!"

"I'll tell you later," Ravi said. "Sounds like we're in demand."

Lizzy looked back at the portrait as they walked upstairs. "I bet *he* wasn't vicious," she said. If anything, the expression in Uncle George's blue eyes was sad and faraway, as if he had been the victim of some terrible event, not its perpetrator.

"Ah, Ravi, Lizzy! Do come and have some tea." Lavinia was sitting opposite the Sams on one of the sofas by the roaring fire as they came in. She aimed her sweetest smile at Ravi. "Did you have a nice lunch?"

114

"Very, thank you, Mrs Abercrombie," Ravi answered. "Lizzy's father is a remarkable man." The Sams looked at each other, suppressing a snigger. "And Rose seems very nice … "

"Rose? … " Lavinia raised an eyebrow.

"She was my art teacher at Knowlesby High," Lizzy explained.

"Oh, a *teacher*!" Aunt Lavinia managed to make it sound as if being a teacher were only one step up from being a poacher.

"Why don't you sit down, Ravi?" Samantha said, patting the sofa beside her. She was wearing a brand-new green jersey, and black mascara on her eyelashes which were fluttering like moths on a windowpane.

"Yah! Why don't you?" drawled Samuel. He wasn't sure whether to be jealous of his sister's obvious interest in Ravi, or pleased that they'd managed to get him to come to Shalimar. In the end, he'd decided on the latter—most of his cronies had been wildly impressed.

Ravi sat nervously next to Samantha as she shot coy glances at him. Lizzy sat next to Aunt Lavinia who took no notice of her at all.

"Maud! Pour the tea for our guest!" Lavinia ordered. Maud Batty had been cowering in a corner with the tea tray. She was wearing the same pinny that she'd been wearing the last time that Lizzy saw her at Christmas.

"Hello, Maud," Lizzy said with a smile as she carried the tray over, the cups rattling. "Long time, no see!"

Maud put the tray down carefully on the low table between the sofas, grinning at Lizzy as she did so.

"So, Ravi," said Lavinia as Maud handed the cups around, "what do you make of our little slice of India?" She gestured lightly with a perfectly manicured hand.

115

"Shalimar, you mean?" Ravi replied. "I think it's a dream. I'd never have expected an extraordinary building like this here … "

"Lizzy's shown you the Durbar Hall, of course? The chandelier is a recent addition—"

"We didn't have time to see everything this morning, Aunt," Lizzy interrupted. "We went to find Josh."

"Josh? … " Lavinia repeated, as if she had never heard his name before.

"Joshua Giddons. You know … "

"Ah, the groom's boy!" Lavinia flashed an apologetic smile at Ravi.

"Do you have servants at your home in India?" Samantha asked.

"I don't know," Ravi replied, "I haven't seen it yet. Dad's only just bought it. But I'm sure there will be a few … "

"Is it a large house?" asked Samuel.

"It's a penthouse apartment, actually. The top three floors of a thirty-storey block."

"A penthouse!" said Lavinia. "How extraordinary! I had no idea that they had such things in India."

Ravi turned his dark eyes on her. "Oh yes! We're quite advanced, you know!" Only Lizzy knew him well enough to detect his sarcasm.

There was a pause for a moment as they finished their tea.

"Why don't I show you the Durbar Hall, Ravi?" cooed Samantha.

"Yah, I'll come too," Samuel said quickly.

"Okay," Ravi said. "Are you coming, Lizzy?"

"Oh no," Samantha said, glancing acidly at Lizzy, "she's had you all morning! It's our turn now." And she bore Ravi out of the room like a trophy, Samuel following behind.

116

"Don't forget to tell him all about the chandelier, darlings!" Lavinia called after them. "And remember, the artist's name is Rajesh Jog ... " She turned to Lizzy. "You know, I think Ravi's taken a real shine to Samantha. But then she is an astonishingly pretty girl. And it's not just the mother in me saying that ... I had lunch with the Ochterlonies last week and Lady Hortensia told me that she thought Samantha was one of—"

"Excuse me, Aunt," Lizzy interrupted, knowing that otherwise she'd never get away. "I've just remembered that I have to call Dad ... "

"Oh!" said Lavinia, as Lizzy got up quickly and headed out of the door. "Oh!" she said again. If there was one thing she hated, it was not having an audience.

Lizzy ran down the stairs two at a time. She wanted to see Josh.

22

ABOUT INDIA

THERE WAS NO ONE AT HOME when she knocked on the door of Stable Cottage. Lizzy scribbled a note to Josh and slid it under the door. She didn't ask him to come round to Shalimar—she knew that he wouldn't want to. When she got back to the house she found Ravi in the entrance hall looking at the oil paintings, trapped between the Sams. He looked hugely relieved when she appeared.

"Oh! It's you again!" Samantha said, not bothering to conceal her disappointment.

Lizzy ignored her. "What did you think of the Durbar Hall?" she asked Ravi.

"Absolutely fantastic!" he replied, detaching himself from the twins and walking over to her. Then, under his breath, he pleaded "Get me away from them! Quick!"

Lizzy thought for a second. "I've just been to Joshua's," she announced brightly, "and he's asked us all over to say hello."

The Sams looked mortified. They'd never been inside Stable Cottage, and had no intention of doing so now. They muttered excuses about having homework to do.

Ravi looked dubious too, but that was because Josh made him nervous.

119

"It's all right," Lizzy whispered to him as the Sams slinked out, "I made that up. You did ask me to get you away from them."

Ravi nodded gratefully. "They were asking me when my father was next in England so that they could invite him to Shalimar. It's all they're interested in."

They left the house and walked down the gravel driveway towards Josh's cottage, just in case the Sams were spying on them.

"Would your Dad like it, do you think?" Lizzy asked.

"Shalimar? He'd love it, of course—who wouldn't? But it's a shame about the occupants. The younger ones, I mean," he added hastily. "Your aunt is charming."

"A penthouse!" Lizzy imitated Lavinia's voice perfectly. "How extraordinary! I'd no idea that they had such things in India."

Ravi chuckled. Lizzy switched to imitating his voice.

"Oh yes! We're quite advanced, you know!"

Ravi convulsed himself laughing. They'd branched off, taking the path towards Maya Lodge, and by the time he had recovered they found themselves on the Brahmin Bridge. The sun was setting over the distant hills, and the Snake Pool reflected the gold and pinks of the sky.

Ravi looked around him and sighed. "He must have been an extraordinary man, your Uncle George. This place really is like a dream."

"You never got around to explaining what he did in India."

Ravi thought for a moment then looked seriously at Lizzy. "You know that *The Lifeline* was originally written in English?"

"Yeah ... "

"Why do you think Shankar Pujari, an Indian, writes in English?"

Lizzy wasn't sure. "I suppose he learnt it at school."

"Exactly," Ravi said, "I was at boarding school for a couple of years in India, before I came to Laythorpe. My parents were keen that I shouldn't lose touch with my roots. Anyway, the school I went to had been built by the British in 1879, and there they taught us in English. I read Shakespeare and Milton; we sat English exams, we played cricket and rugby—at least the others did—drank tea and ate with knives and forks. I said my goodbyes in English when term ended, took the train home on railway lines built by the British, across British bridges over British irrigation canals, and when I arrived in Mumbai it was at Victoria Terminus, the biggest station in Asia … "

" … Built by the British?"

"Correct. Built by the British."

"But what's that got to do with Uncle George?"

"He was employed by the East India Company. They were a company of merchants originally, but in the end they ran India as a country. They introduced all those things that were so much part of my life in India. Plus a lot of other things like the legal system and universities … "

"So they did have their good points, after all. Like the Normans bringing their fancy French manners to Britain."

"Yes, exactly," Ravi smiled. "*Pardon, fair damsel, would'st thou dance with me?* and all that courtly stuff … "

"Not a hope in hell, Ravi," Lizzy said. "You've got two left feet."

"Anyway," he laughed. "After 1858 the East India Company was taken over by the British Crown."

"That's when Uncle George left, wasn't it?" Lizzy said.

"Yes. It may be just a coincidence, but that year saw an uprising against the British in the north. You call it the Mutiny—we call it the First War of Independence. You see, a lot of Indians hated the British and wanted them to leave."

"Mutiny?" Lizzy asked, puzzled. "But that's when soldiers won't follow orders, isn't it?"

"Yeah. You see, most of the East India Company's army were Indians. Sepoys they were called. For them being a soldier was a job, and the Company paid well for their services."

"So the British used Indians to conquer India?" Lizzy was astonished.

"Yeah. Complicated, isn't it? Uncle George was the Resident, the East India Company's representative in Junagadh, an independent state—there were lots in India in those days. The Nawab could run his state exactly how he liked, except he couldn't go to war on his neighbours—the Company didn't want anyone stirring up trouble that could disrupt their trade. After all, they were there to make money. And George was there to make sure the Nawab obeyed the Company's rules."

As she paused to look at George's portrait on the staircase when she was making her way up to bed later that night, Lizzy found it hard to imagine that her swashbuckling uncle had anything to do with making sure people obeyed boring rules. She thought he looked more like a pirate than a policeman.

When she finally lay down in the four-poster, she left the bedside light on and marvelled at the murals, and the starry night sky that was painted on the inside of the dome. She imagined that she was Uncle George, travelling the long road to Junagadh to become Resident there. Would he have seen the procession of pilgrims that the picture showed? Would he have seen the temples on the mountains in the distance? Would he have paused and set up camp by the stream, and heard the women singing as they washed their clothes on the rocks? Would he have smelt the smoke from the dried dung fires in the village? Would he …

Before she knew it, Lizzy was fast asleep.

She dreamt of India.

23

A NIGHTMARE AND AN INVITATION

SHE WAS INSIDE A DARK, crowded temple—candlelight flickered dimly on yellowed marble walls that seemed to breathe in and out like the lungs of an enormous beast … People on all sides pressed in on her, straining to look at something which she couldn't see, their faces hidden beneath their hooded robes—she was trapped … unable to move—they swayed from side to side to a mad riot of metallic rhythms growing ever more frenzied, ever more intense—the infernal clanging of a thousand demon anvils, pulsing with a frantic energy which seemed to crush her head like a vice. She screamed with her last remaining breath …

An exhausted Lizzy knocked on the door of Stable Cottage the following morning.

"Now then," Josh grinned as he peered over her shoulder. "What have you done with Clever Clogs?"

"Is anyone else in?" Lizzy smiled wanly, and Josh's eyes narrowed as he scrutinised her.

"No … are you all right, Lizzy?"

"Not really."

125

They went into the Cottage and while Josh made her a cup of tea, Lizzy told him about her nightmare. She was still shaken, and had only slept fitfully.

"Did you tell Ravi?" Josh asked.

"No. And I haven't said anything about the curse, obviously. He doesn't know about that."

Josh nodded, secretly pleased. He jumped up and consulted an almanac that was sitting on a bookshelf. After leafing through it for a moment he shut it, a look of concern on his face.

"What is it?" Lizzy asked.

"Just as I thought … last night was the full moon!"

"I didn't see it."

"You wouldn't—it was too cloudy. But that doesn't seem to make much difference, does it? There's definitely something about you and moon … "

"You think so?" Lizzy shuddered as if someone had walked on her grave. They looked at each other blankly.

There wasn't any point in dwelling on it, so they talked about other things while they were drinking their tea. Josh was his usual quiet self, but eventually she managed to get out of him the fact that Susan Birkinshaw had been suspended from Knowlesby Grammar for a week after swearing at a teacher and Bryony Adamson was going steady with Kevin Slaymaker from the village.

"He dumped Delice Tasker just after New Year," Josh commented. "Was she mad!"

Lizzy managed a grin. Her old enemies seemed so far away now.

"What are you doing for the Easter Holidays?" she asked.

"Doing? Why, I'll be here, won't I?" he said, puzzled. "Won't you?"

"Of course I will," Lizzy reassured him. "And we can do lots of things together. I've been dreaming of going to The Plaice Place since I went away to Laythorpe—they're all into salads and healthy eating there."

"Yuk!" They both grinned.

"Have you seen anything of Mabel Corker?" Lizzy asked.

"No. But then you wanted me to forget all about her, didn't you?"

She smiled at him affectionately. It was as if she'd never been away.

Lizzy walked back to Shalimar and into the entrance hall.

"Shhhh … " Samantha hissed at her. In the hall at the bottom of the staircase Ravi was pacing back and forth and talking nineteen to the dozen into his mobile phone.

"Yeah, it's great here, you'd love it, it's really amazing … Yeah? … "

"Why are you listening in on his call?" Lizzy said.

"Shhh … " Samuel hissed.

"It's very rude!" she said.

"It's his father," Samantha said. "KK Chandra!"

" … in Junagadh. I've been going through it with her Dad … It's incredible! … Yeah? … No! … Really? … Does Shankar know that? … He does? … "

Even Lizzy couldn't help pricking up her ears at the mention of the name of the writer of *The Lifeline*.

" … No reason why not, if he lets her … It would be great! Thanks, Dad! I'll call you later … Bye!"

Ravi walked into the entrance hall.

"Oh! You're back, Lizzy!" he said, surprised. "I was just talking to my Dad. You know I told you that they're going to be doing the location shoots for *The Lifeline* near Junagadh, where Shankar based some of the scenes in the book?" The Sams' eyes were out on stalks. This was just too much! Ravi made it seem as if knowing Shankar was perfectly normal.

"Anyway, I told him about your Uncle George … and Shankar said—"

"Shankar was with your Dad?" Lizzy interrupted incredulously.

"Sure. They're working very closely together on the film. Shankar's a real history nut. Especially the history of that part of Gujarat, so Dad tells me. That's where he's from. And, get this, he's heard of your Uncle George!"

"What!" It seemed unbelievable to Lizzy. The Sams looked on, puzzled. They'd never taken the slightest interest in their forebears, and had no idea why Uncle George was suddenly the centre of attention.

"Anyway," Ravi continued. "I'm going there to stay with the film crew on location for a week or so while I'm in Mumbai during the Easter holidays. Dad's had it all organised for months as a surprise for me."

"Wow! Lucky you!" Lizzy said.

Ravi suddenly looked far less confident. "Well actually, Lizzy," he replied, blushing, "he said I could invite you, too. If you'd like to come, that is."

Lizzy's face lit up with pleasure. "Wow! I'd love to!"

With a howl of despair Samantha ran out of the room. Samuel went white, looked at Lizzy with an expression of measureless hatred, and followed her.

128

"That's really going to make you popular round here," Ravi added with a broad grin. "We'd better ask your dad."

They headed straight to Maya Lodge.

"That's an amazing coincidence," Lizzy said as they walked down the drive. "Shankar knowing about Uncle George and all that … "

"Yeah," Ravi said. " It's funny—Shankar once told me that you can't afford to put as many coincidences in stories as there are in real life 'cos no one will believe you … But it's not even that surprising, really. He knows just about everything there is to know about the Junagadh area, and very few Brits made it there. But it's well known in India because of the *Mahabharata* and the *Ramayana*."

"The sacred Hindu texts?"

"Yeah," Ravi said. "Anyway near Junagadh is a mountain where the exiles in the *Mahabharata* went, so there are lots of pilgrims and temples … "

"Wow!"

"Yeah, we should have some fun there."

Rose car was parked outside Maya Lodge, and she was chatting to Lizzy's father in the sitting room. She'd driven over specially to see Lizzy again—so she said.

Lizzy was too full of her own news to resent Rose always being around. Unable to contain herself for an instant, she told them about the invitation she'd received from Ravi's father to go to India. Henry was dubious at first, but when Ravi told him they would be accompanied on the flight both there and back by his mother, he was partly reassured. He finally gave his agreement, as long as he could meet Ravi's mother beforehand.

"So you'll be following in the footsteps of Uncle George," Henry said. "How exciting!"

Rose beamed. "Wonderful, Lizzy!"

"It is, isn't it?" But Lizzy thought sadly of her mother, and how excited she'd been about their plans to go to India together. That was not be—but it seemed that her destiny was to go to India nonetheless.

Ravi was equally pleased. He'd often been lonely in the past during school holidays, and it would be the first time he'd actually had a friend to stay with him. And her Uncle George's connection with Junagadh would make it all the more fun for both Lizzy and him.

Henry asked Ravi all about Mumbai, and started to get quite envious of Lizzy's good fortune. They were all making so much commotion, chattering animatedly and making plans, that only Lizzy heard the knock on the door. She remembered that she'd invited Josh to come round that afternoon and she jumped up to open it.

"Now then, Lizzy," Josh said, listening to the noise coming from the living room as he tied Benjy to the bench outside. "Has someone won the lottery?"

"Better than that," Lizzy grinned, and proceeded to fill him in on what had happened. He reacted in his usual low-key way, but Lizzy could tell that he was very pleased for her.

"It means I won't be here for much of the Easter hols, though," she said.

He smiled ruefully. "Yeah, well, I'll manage some'ow, Lizzy."

24

MUMBAI

KERUUUMP!

A noise like a clap of thunder on the roof of the four-wheel drive jolted Lizzy abruptly out of her sleep. She awoke feeling totally disoriented, her heart thumping.

"What was that?" she exclaimed.

"Good shot!" yelled Ravi.

"Bloody cricketing!" muttered Ravi's mother.

Lizzy wondered where on earth she was. The car had stopped by the pavement, and beyond the iron railings of a park she could see lots of young men dressed in white playing cricket. In the distance was a huge Victorian bell tower which dimly reminded her of Big Ben. Other imposing old buildings surrounded the park.

"Are we still in London?" she asked, rubbing her eyes, and blushed when the others burst out laughing.

"This is Mumbai, Lizzy—you were asleep!" Ravi's mother turned to her with a warm smile. She wore a sari which showed off her slim brown midriff and long, delicate forearms which were covered in gold bangles. She was called Kitten, a name that made Lizzy want to giggle every time she heard it.

Ravi opened the door and as he got out a wave of warm, damp air hit her. The cricket ball had bounced off the roof of the car into the road and a barefoot Indian boy had managed to find it despite the frenetic traffic. Ravi fished in his pocket, handed the boy a grubby bank note and tossed the ball to the young man in cricket whites who had come to the railings to retrieve it. They exchanged a few words.

"It's the University second team batting against Rajput College seconds," Ravi explained as he climbed back into the car. "That was a fantastic six!"

Lizzy looked at him in surprise. "I didn't know you liked cricket!"

"It's in the Indian genes, Lizzy," he replied as the driver eased his way back into the traffic giving short blasts on his horn. "Even those who don't play love to watch."

"But it's an English game, isn't it?"

"Originally, yes, but when India threw the British out at Independence, we kept your bats and balls. Now we're better at it than you are … "

Within a few moments of setting off, Lizzy was asleep again.

She had hardly slept at all during the overnight flight. When they arrived at Mumbai airport it was already early morning, even though Lizzy's watch told her that it should be the middle of the night. Her legs felt like lead and she hardly knew if she was coming or going. Ravi's father's driver, dressed in a smart blue uniform and wearing a chauffeur's cap, met them after customs and taking their luggage led them through the bustle, while Lizzy mechanically tagged along. She sank gratefully into the leather seats of the four-wheel drive as the air conditioning fought off the sweltering heat outside.

Other than the brief rude awakening by the cricket ball, she slept all the way from the airport to the building where KK and Kitten lived, and the next thing she knew was that Ravi was shaking her shoulder and saying "Wake up, Lizzy, we're here!"

'Here' was a concrete underground car park. A man in a white uniform greeted Kitten with a salute, opened the car doors, and they got out onto a red carpet leading to the lifts. A brass plaque by one of the lift doors read 'Penthouse Only'.

"You have your own lift?" Lizzy asked Kitten incredulously.

"The architect insisted on it, thank God. Imagine if we had to stop at other floors every time we went up or down! It'd take all day!"

When the doors opened into the penthouse apartment, Lizzy gasped.

"Cool!" Ravi murmured, as they stepped out and gazed around in wonder. Everything was made of steel and glass, and huge plasma screens were built into the walls over pale wood flooring. Enormous windows overlooked a great sweeping bay, and ferries plied their way back and forth across the sparkling blue sea. They were so high up it was as if the rest of the city scarcely existed.

"KK—Ravi's father—is very keen on video art," Kitten explained, pointing at the flat screens everywhere which showed all sorts of curious moving images. The walls seemed to be alive. "I can see you're still half-asleep, Lizzy," she continued, "so after you've unpacked, why not spend the rest of the day by the pool relaxing? We're going to the launch party for the start of the filming of *The Lifeline* this evening … We'll be up late, so you should get as much rest as you can this afternoon."

When she saw her room, Lizzy could hardly believe her eyes. The view took up the whole of one wall, but it was the gadgets that got her attention. She could press a button by her bedside to open and close the curtains; another series of switches controlled all the lights; then she pressed another button, and a panel on the wall slid back to reveal another huge screen. Using the wireless keyboard she could sit on her bed and connect to films, music, e-mails and the Internet. She tracked down the latest Heart 2 Heart album and played it as she unpacked her suitcase. When she took her spongebag into the marble bathroom, the music played through speakers in there too.

This must be the coolest bedroom on the planet! she thought. Except perhaps for her favourite one at Shalimar.

She went next door to Ravi's room to tell him about it, and found him sitting on his bed tapping away at a keyboard, web sites displayed on his own enormous TV.

"Dad's a technology nut," he explained. "He had all this stuff installed when they were building the place. Apparently it's the same by the pool, too."

"Where is the pool?" Lizzy asked.

Ravi pointed at the ceiling. "On the roof. Dad's particularly pleased with it, he told me. So I expect it'll be amazing … "

It was.

The whole of the roof area was an immaculate garden with gravel walkways covered with trellises of roses, and shady areas with cushioned sun loungers to lie on. The pool was at the edge and the blue of the water seemed to melt into the sky.

Lizzy walked around, taking in the spectacular views over the city and the ocean.

After they had changed into their swimsuits, Ravi fiddled with the controls of a smaller flat-screen TV. "I see you were listening to Heart 2 Heart in your room, Lizzy. I'll start it where you left off … "

As the music played through hidden speakers, Ravi dived into the pool. A moment later his face reappeared, grinning, and he shook his head, sending a spray of water from his jet-black hair.

"I don't believe this!" he cried, thrilled.

Nor did Lizzy. As she and Ravi swam back and forwards, Lizzy felt as if they were floating high above the earth with nothing but the clouds for company. She lay on her back and paddled lazily.

"*All we need is here and now* … " Heart 2 Heart sang the chorus of her favourite track. " … *Every now and then.*"

25

A BOLLYWOOD PARTY

"Lizzy, this is Shankar Pujari," said Ravi's father at the party that evening. "He's been very keen to meet you."

She recognised the author of *The Lifeline* immediately. Hardly a day passed without his photograph appearing in a newspaper or magazine, his thin, thoughtful face beneath a shock of white hair. He was taller in real life than she expected, and leaner. He smiled, his brown eyes shining with intelligence.

"So KK, this is the descendant of the illustrious 'Lion' Abercrombie you told me about?" he asked, taking Lizzy's hand and bowing slightly. "I am delighted to make your acquaintance."

Lizzy was entirely tongue-tied.

KK helped her out.

"Shankar knows more about the history of Gujarat than anyone, Lizzy," he explained. "And he's a great admirer of George Abercrombie."

"Without him the lions would now be extinct—although the Nawab took the credit, of course," Shankar said.

Lizzy nodded as if she knew what he was talking about.

KK looked at her. He was smaller than Ravi, stocky, and full of restless energy and good humour.

"You know about the lions of the Gir, don't you?" he asked gently.

Lizzy started to nod again, but then shook her head.

"Well, it will be my pleasure to tell you all about them when we sail to Somnath," Shankar assured her. A young woman tried to catch his attention. "Wait a moment, Sunila," he told her sharply, dismissing her with a wave.

KK was also trying to fend off people wanting to ask him questions or get his orders. It had been like this since Lizzy had arrived at the party, but he had made as much time as he could to be especially welcoming to her.

"Sail?" asked Lizzy, finally finding her tongue.

"Didn't Ravi tell you?" KK asked. "I've hired a yacht as a back-up production office, and we'll all be sailing in it from Mumbai the day after tomorrow across to Gujarat. Somnath is on the coast there."

"And we'll have plenty of time to talk then, Lizzy," Shankar added. "As you can appreciate, this is not exactly the ideal occasion." He took her hand and said goodbye as Sunila again approached nervously.

"Goodbye," Lizzy managed to say politely. *I've met Shankar Pujari!* she thought. She almost had to pinch herself. *And he's a fan of Uncle George!* She looked around her as Shankar and KK were borne away in a wave of excited photographers, journalists and hangers-on.

The party was in the garden of a large luxury hotel by the sea in Bandra, an hour's drive from the city centre. As Lizzy had entered with Ravi and Kitten, she'd been dazzled. The word 'WELCOME' was spelt out in fairy lights on the lawn, more lights spiralled around the trunks of every tall palm tree, and hundreds of candles glimmered on the tables spread around the garden. The smell of jasmine and the sound of crickets filled the night air.

After the thrill of meeting Shankar, Lizzy found herself rapidly getting more and more tired. Ravi kept being whisked off to meet old acquaintances of his father's, and although Kitten tried introducing Lizzy to glamorous Indian movie starlets, none of them seemed remotely interested in her. They all spent their time looking over her shoulder in case they saw someone important to talk to. One didn't even bother to finish her sentence before rushing off when she spotted a handsome young man with blond dreadlocks surrounded by a group of starlets, all giggling girlishly. Lizzy thought she recognised him from somewhere.

She wandered off towards the bar, asked for a lime juice and soda, then took it to a table under a palm tree at the end of the garden. When she sat down, she was surprised to see a dog lying on the grass at the base of the tree, his watchful brown eyes looking up at her with interest. He was like one of those breeds she had seen in tomb paintings from ancient Egypt.

She patted the grass beside her, called him, and the dog sprang to his feet and came over, his tail wagging.

Within moments he and Lizzy were firm friends, and she was so busy petting him that she didn't notice the blond-dreadlocked young man she had seen earlier standing by the table watching her, an amused smile playing on his coffee-coloured features.

"His name's Kiva," he said. The young man held out his hand. "I'm Johnny, Johnny Cairo."

"Lizzy Abercrombie," replied Lizzy, holding out hers.

"Johnny, man!" A voice called across the lawn.

Johnny raised his arm in response, and said, "We've got to go, Lizzy. See ya!" He untied Kiva and made his way towards the entrance, Kiva following close by.

Johnny Cairo ... she thought. *There's an old reggae singer called Jimmy Cairo who married a Swedish model. That could explain those blond dreadlocks* ...

Lizzy sighed. Kitten was dragging over yet another beautiful starlet to meet her.

All she could think about was bed.

26

LOST AND FOUND

LIZZY WAS STILL HORRIBLY tired at eleven o'clock the next morning when they were being driven through the mad Mumbai traffic to the railway station to meet Ravi's cousin, Kiran. She fiddled idly on the keyboard of the mobile that Kitten had given her, with instructions that the phone numbers of the penthouse and all the family had already been programmed into it for her.

They had eaten breakfast on the terrace and afterwards Lizzy had scribbled a couple of postcards, one to Josh and the other to her father. Kitten had given her stamps for them, and told her she'd be able to post them at the station.

"You know I told you about Victoria Terminus?" Ravi said, as a vast Victorian building came into view.

"You said it was enormous," Lizzy remembered. "Is that it?"
"Yup. But it's been renamed Chhatrapati Shivaji Terminus after a famous Maratha freedom fighter ... "

Lizzy attempted vainly to repeat the name.

" ... but people still call it 'VT'," Ravi continued.
"I'm not surprised."
"Three million people use it every day."
"Three million people?" Lizzy's mind boggled.

And it seemed to her that at least one million of them were at the station when they got there—she had never been anywhere so crowded in her life. The driver dropped them off at the entrance, and they fought their way inside through the crowds. Ravi was looking forward to seeing Kiran.

"She's over from the States," he explained. "I haven't seen her for years, but I bet you'll like her."

"Is she coming with us to Gujarat?" Lizzy asked.

"No, she's staying with her aunt on Malabar Hill for a few days. But first we're taking her to my mother's lunch party at the Taj Hotel." He looked at an arrivals information board. "Platform Six," he announced decisively. "Come on, follow me."

"Hang on a second … " Lizzy said. She'd spotted a bright-red postbox, just like the one in the main street of Nethermoorside. She walked over and dropped her postcards through the slot.

As she turned back someone in the fast moving crowd bumped into her, and her bag fell to the ground. She scrambled to retrieve it, and when she looked up again she thought she saw the back of Ravi's head moving away through the crowds. Trying to catch up with him was like swimming in a huge river with currents flowing in several different directions at once.

It's so crowded! she thought, struggling to control a sudden wave of panic. Was that Ravi turning left ahead of her?

She followed the bobbing head of dark hair, but to her dismay when the boy turned round it wasn't Ravi.

She suddenly remembered her mobile phone and reached into her pocket for it.

It had gone …

Panic tightened its grip. Lost among three million people! she thought, horrified. She forced herself to take a deep breath—Ravi must be looking for her, surely?

She could see a sign to the ticket hall—maybe the ticket sellers spoke English? The hall was like the nave of a great cathedral—there were scores of ticket booths, and a long line at each one. She stood in a queue to wait, but it moved agonisingly slowly.

There was a plump woman just ahead of her.

"Excuse me," Lizzy asked hesitantly. "Do you speak English?"

"English! Very good!" she replied with a warm smile.

"I'm lost," Lizzy said with a great sigh of relief. "I wonder if you could help me?"

The woman turned to the neighbouring man in the queue.

"English!" she stated proudly, pointing at Lizzy.

"Yes," Lizzy continued. "I've lost my friend and … "

"Ah, English!" the neighbour repeated, looking at her. He offered her a biscuit from a shiny foil packet.

She realised that they had no idea what she was talking about, and stumbled back towards the platforms. Managing to find a clear space just by a huge stone pillar, she leant back against it. She was near to tears.

Just then she felt something nudging her thigh. Startled, she looked down and saw the trusting brown eyes of a dog, nuzzling her with his nose and wagging his tail in greeting.

"Kiva!" She recognised him immediately.

"Hey, there!" Lizzy looked up: Johnny Cairo was standing over her, wearing a white T-shirt with "JOHNNY'S COOL!" written in red, green and gold letters.

143

Lizzy was deeply relieved to see a friendly face. She told him in a faltering voice how she had got separated from Ravi, and how she'd lost her mobile with all the numbers, and that the only thing she could remember was that she was supposed to be going out for lunch.

"Where?" Johnny asked.

"I think he said the Raj Hotel ... "

"The Taj? ... "

"That's it!"

Punching a number into his mobile phone, Johnny spoke to someone at the hotel. "Okay that's fixed, Mrs Chandra will know you're safe. I'll take you ... Follow me!"

He led her through the station, down a long crowded passage and out into the bright sunlight. An old Enfield motorbike was parked by the pavement. He swung his leg over the saddle.

"Hop on!" he ordered Kiva, who jumped onto the petrol tank. "And you too!"

"I've never ridden a motorbike before," Lizzy said as she clambered on behind him.

Johnny glanced down. "Put your feet on those rests. You don't want to burn yourself on the exhaust."

He kick-started the bike and roared off into the wide avenue clogged with traffic. He weaved expertly through the mêlée of buses, cars and tiny yellow-and-black taxis, leaning from one side to the other as they whizzed along.

The warm, humid wind rushed through her hair as they passed a stately elephant walking by the side of the road. Smells overwhelmed her—hot tarmac, spices and a faint whiff of rotten eggs. Lush green tropical plants seemed to burst from everywhere. Graceful women walked in their brilliant saris like flocks of parrots past pavement stalls

144

swamped with plastic toys in startling pinks, oranges and greens. Indian film music flooded onto the streets from open shop fronts selling heaps of glittering bangles. At every set of traffic lights begging children held out their hands, shouting, "Hello! Hello!"

The life of Mumbai swirled and whirled around Lizzy like a fairground carousel.

"What do you think of this crazy town, then?" Johnny shouted to her over his shoulder.

"It's insane, I love it!" Lizzy shouted. "Sensory overload!"

Johnny laughed. "I guess you're right."

A moment later he halted the bike by a long stretch of beach, the sea sparkling in the bright sunlight.

"Chowpatty Beach," Johnny announced. "Jump off and we'll take a quick look. Guard the bike, Kiva!"

It was strange to be on a beach in the middle of such a huge city. They walked across the broad swathe of sand where thousands of families ate picnics laid out on mats. Vendors wandered around selling corncobs and balloons, and excited children blew streams of bubbles that glinted in the sun.

They were just heading back towards the bike when a thin, reedy sound from a flute caught their attention. They edged through the crowd to see what was going on and Lizzy jumped in alarm at the sight of a cobra uncoiling from a basket at her feet.

As they pushed their way back through, she felt a tug at her sleeve and looked down to see the hollow staring eyes of a wizened old man holding out a begging bowl. Johnny gave him some rumpled notes, and Lizzy was horrified to see stumps where his legs should have been as he pushed himself along on a makeshift wooden trolley.

Johnny steered her quickly away. She was more relieved than ever that he had found her.

"How did you happen to be at the station?" Lizzy asked him as they set off on the bike.

"I was seeing a friend onto a train ... someone I work with."

"What do you do?"

"I'm training at a new film company, you know, computer special effects and all that. My Dad got me the gig—India's the coming place and I want to catch the wave."

27

THE TAJ

JOHNNY STOPPED THE MOTORBIKE outside a vast old building overlooking the sea.

"This is it," said Johnny. "The Taj Mahal hotel."

Lizzy looked up in wonder. It looked more like a palace.

A turbaned man in immaculate traditional Indian dress opened the door for them. Inside the pleasant cool of the air-conditioning hit them after the heat of the city.

"We're looking for Mrs Chandra's party," Johnny told the concierge.

"Yes, sir, they're at the pool side." He led them through the entrance hallway, with its grand staircase which was three times as big as that at Shalimar. It seemed to ascend for at least five floors, and Lizzy was so busy looking up that she nearly bumped into two Arab sheikhs dressed in long brilliant white robes.

As she and Johnny stepped out onto an elegant veranda, Kitten came flying towards them, the scarf of her turquoise sari billowing behind.

"Oh God, Lizzy! It's you!" she cried as she wrapped her in her arms. "I was so relieved when I got the message! We were so worried about you! What happened? Ravi rang to say you'd disappeared! He'd got half the railway police looking for you! I am furious with him—how could he lose you like that! Oh God, anything could have happened! Anything!" She wiped a tear from her eye with a corner of her scarf.

"It's all right, Mrs Chandra, honestly," Lizzy insisted. She was far less upset than Kitten, it seemed. "This is Johnny Cairo. He brought me here."

Johnny had been standing modestly to one side, and moved forwards to shake Kitten's hand. "Hi! I was at your husband's party last night—that's how I know Lizzy."

Kitten hung onto his hand and looked gratefully at Johnny. "So you're the knight in shining armour? Oh God, where did you find her?"

Johnny quickly explained how the mobile must have been stolen and how he'd found Lizzy lost in the station. Kitten accompanied the tale with gasps of astonishment and horror, clutched Lizzy's hand to her chest, and said "Oh God!" at least twenty times.

Ravi arrived soon after, looking distinctly sheepish.

He was with the most beautiful Indian girl Lizzy had yet seen. She was about sixteen, with long legs and an impossibly slender waist.

They both came straight over to where Lizzy was standing with Johnny.

"I am so, so sorry, Lizzy," Ravi apologised. "Will you ever forgive me?"

"You're forgiven already," Lizzy smiled sweetly. "But I'm afraid I've lost the mobile … "

Ravi realised he hadn't introduced his cousin.

"This is Kiran. Kiran, this is Lizzy."

"Pleased to meet you," Lizzy said as they shook hands.

"Oh my God, I'm like sooo pleased to meet you too, it was like, when I met Ravi at the station, I was like just sooo impressed with him, I haven't seen him in years, and he like told me all about you, only like you weren't there! And like Ravi, he was soooo frantic, I said Oh my God, like cool it, Ravi, duh! ... "

Kiran droned on in her horrible nasal voice for what seemed ages while Ravi squirmed with embarrassment. It was only when Johnny interrupted to tell Lizzy that he had to go that she stopped for a second.

"Good bye, Johnny," Lizzy murmured shyly. "And thanks for everything ... "

"No problem!" He handed her a card. "Anytime you want just give me a call ... " With that he turned and left.

Kiran peered over Lizzy's shoulder at the card.

" ... Oh my God that was like Johnny Cairo? Jimmy Cairo's son? And he's like, your friend? He is just like soooo totally, way past cool."

"I know," said Lizzy. "It says so on his T-shirt."

28

ALL ABOARD

LIZZY LEANT BACK contentedly in the comfortable chair on the rear deck of the *Jupiter* and gazed at the blaze of stars above her in the hot tropical night and at the moon reflected in the swelling sea. The yacht was much bigger than she had imagined—in fact it was more like a ship. It had two decks, plenty of cabins all with their own bathrooms, and a kitchen which produced endless amounts of delicious food.

KK had spent nearly all the day on his satellite phone or closeted below with Shankar, so she and Ravi had hardly seen them since they'd set sail. But just as Lizzy was about to suggest that they play a game of cards, Shankar appeared, followed by a young Indian woman whom Lizzy recognised from the party.

"May I join you?" Shankar asked courteously. She thought how elegant he looked in his flowing Indian clothes. "You remember Sunila, I'm sure," he continued. "She's my assistant, which means of course that she does all the hard work ... It looks as if KK will be talking to his producers in London for the next hour, so this might be a good opportunity for me to tell you a bit more about George Abercrombie, and for you to tell me what you know. You see," he announced, leaning back in his chair to deliver his bombshell, "I'm thinking of basing a character in my next book on him!"

Uncle George might be in a book by Shankar Pujari! Lizzy nodded dumbly as he continued, the fingertips of his thin hands touching lightly.

"What I find so interesting about George Abercrombie was that he persuaded the Nawab of Junagadh to forbid lion-hunting in his kingdom, and he was well ahead of his time in doing so. All over India many of the native rulers and the Britishers alike hunted most animals to virtual extinction and most didn't give a damn. George was the first conservationist in our country—that's why I call him 'Lion' Abercrombie. He saved the lions."

'Lion' Abercrombie! Lizzy had wondered why he had called him that. She felt very proud—she'd always known that Uncle George was something special.

"He was obviously a remarkable person," Shankar added, "But I need to get a better sense of what kind of man he was—to put flesh on the bones. So, Lizzy, what can you tell me about him?"

Now that she knew he would be interested in what she had to say, Lizzy babbled away merrily, recounting everything she could remember about the whole saga from his marriage to the heiress Penelope to his final disappearance. She was too carried away to notice that Sunila was making a note of everything she said …

"And so he was never heard of again!" Lizzy finally finished exultantly.

The steady gaze of Shankar's brown eyes didn't leave her face for an instant. "Curious," he observed, and added casually, "I suppose he must have been the only one of your family to … depart, shall we say, in unusual circumstances?"

"Oh, no," Lizzy enthused, telling Shankar about the dramatic events in the family. "There's even talk about a curse … the curse of Shalimar!"

As soon as she mentioned the curse, she wished she hadn't. It wasn't just an exciting story—it had killed her mother.

"You never told me about this!" Ravi complained.

Shankar fell into a thoughtful silence.

The next afternoon the yacht finally moored off Somnath, where a large white building on a low cliff overlooked the sea.

"That's the Temple of the Moon," KK explained. "The most sacred of the twelve Shiva Jyotirlingas in India—pilgrims come from all over. There'll be a ceremony later to celebrate the full moon. I'm meeting some of the crew on that hillside over there. We're going to be filming an establishing shot of the full moon rising from the sea over the Temple. Why don't you stay here and swim—then Shankar could take you along to the ceremony—if that's okay with you, Shankar?"

"Of course!" Shankar agreed. "It's well worth a visit. There has been a temple on the site since ancient times, repeatedly destroyed by conquerors or earthquakes, but always rebuilt to the original plan. The present building dates from the nineteen fifties."

"Won't they mind me being at the ceremony?" Lizzy asked.

"Not at all " he answered with a smile. "Hinduism is a very inclusive religion. Everyone is welcome."

Lizzy and Ravi spent the rest of the day diving from a platform at the stern into the blue sea which was as warm as a swimming pool. The sun was already starting to go down by the time they went to shower and dress.

Ravi went down to find Shankar in his cabin. He came back on deck a minute later.

"Shankar doesn't want to come—he's not feeling too good," he said. "But he's told one of the crew to take us ashore straight away."

They jumped into the small tender and the boatman whizzed it across the sea, the crests of the gentle waves glistening in the sunlight. As they glided onto the pebble beach below the temple. they could hear the sound of distant chanting.

They climbed the steep marble steps that led up the cliff to a courtyard, where huge crowds of pilgrims were converging on the temple in the last rays of the setting sun.

As they left their sandals with thousands of others piled outside, Lizzy wondered if she'd ever see them again. They were swept through the elaborate doorway by the jostling throng—the heat and intense smell of sweat and incense suffocated her. No-one could move. Then she heard the pulsing percussion, a metallic cacophony which chilled her to the marrow. She would have recognised it anywhere— it was the same frenzied rhythmic clanking that she had heard in her nightmare at Shalimar! She started to panic, breathing fast as the music began to increase in pace. The crowd pressed forwards, straining to watch the priest perform the ceremony in front of the six-armed idol of the Moon God. A mesmerising light glimmered in the middle of its forehead, then the walls seemed to press in on Lizzy as the music got louder and faster ...

154

"I've got to get out of here!" she shouted to Ravi.

Somehow she managed to force her way back out through the mass of pilgrims, and by the time Ravi caught up she was sitting against a wall outside taking deep breaths. The moonlight bleached her face to a deathly pallor. Ravi squatted down beside her.

"Are you okay?" he asked.

"I think so," Lizzy replied. "You're going to think I'm crazy, but I've been here before ... "

"What do you mean?" Ravi asked, puzzled.

"In a nightmare. When we were at Shalimar on the full moon. The same music, the same temple, everything ... "

"That really *is* weird," Ravi said, shaking his head in disbelief.

The ceremony had ended and pilgrims were streaming out of the temple, making their way to their nearby lodgings. Lizzy and Ravi walked in silence down to the beach, and the boatman took them back to the *Jupiter*.

As they clambered on board, they found Shankar on deck, smoking a cigarette and looking across the water towards the Temple.

"Are you feeling better?" Ravi asked him.

"What?" he said. "Oh yes—fine, thank you. How was the ceremony?"

"Pretty intense, actually," Lizzy said. "Total déjà vu ... "

29

A MYSTERY

I T WAS COLD AND RAINING, and he didn't have a coat. Josh was fed up.

He had just gone through the Shalimar gates on his way from Nethermoorside to Stable Cottage when the little Fiat drove up, and Rose wound the window down.

"Hello, Joshua," she smiled. "Do you want a lift?"

"Yes please, Miss," he said gratefully and opened the door. There was a neat pile of letters and files on the front seat.

"Just put them on the back seat," Rose suggested. Josh picked the pile up and opened the back door quickly to avoid the papers getting splattered with rain. But a few of the letters at the top slid onto the floor as he put them on the seat.

"Sorry," he mumbled, and picked them up. He couldn't help noticing one of the letters was addressed in Rose's bold handwriting.

MABEL CORKER
ROOM 23
GREENLAWNS RETIREMENT HOME
KNOWLESBY YO7 4NE

What's Rose doing writing to Mabel? he wondered to himself as he got in next to her.

"Are you missing Lizzy?" Rose asked chattily as they set off.

"I had a postcard," Josh responded, busy thinking about Rose and Mabel.

"So did Henr—her father. She seems to be having a good time."

"Yup."

They drove on in silence.

"I'll take you home," Rose said as they passed Maya Lodge.

"Thanks."

She dropped him off outside Stable Cottage, and Josh watched with a puzzled frown as she went back down the drive.

30

ON LOCATION

THE CAST AND CREW of *The Lifeline* stayed in a safari camp at the edge of the Gir Forest. Lizzy had her own tent with a bathroom and air-conditioning, and they all met for meals in a huge open sided-marquee overlooking a river.

Shankar had assured them initially that he would take them to Junagadh and show them the places connected with Uncle George at some stage during their stay on the film set, but the promised trip failed to materialise. Eventually Lizzy gave up thinking about it, and concentrated on enjoying her rides in the magnificent teak forest instead.

It was just as well that she had been able to go riding because she had found out very soon that watching people make films was rather dull. Every shot took hours to set up and light; technicians ran thick cables everywhere and efficient women with clipboards rushed back and forth. Finally the actors would repeat their line or two over and over until KK was happy, then they'd retreat from the heat to their air-conditioned trailers and wait until they were called for the next shot. Lizzy decided that however glamorous being a film star might seem, it was an extremely boring job.

Luckily, as soon as KK had learnt that she was a keen rider he had introduced Lizzy to Vijay, the man who looked after the five Kathiwari horses which were going to be appear in the film. They were the local horses that had been bred in India for many centuries. She'd ridden out every day with Vijay in the dense, mountainous forest while Ravi remained in his tent glued to his computer.

On one of their last mornings on the set, the girl who did the riding scenes for the actress playing the part of Sita had fallen off her horse and broken her arm, throwing KK into a furious temper because the accident would hold up the filming for days. A few hours later he happened to spot a sun-tanned Lizzy cantering back to the stables with Vijay, her long dark hair flowing free. Slapping his forehead with the palm of his hand, he shouted theatrically, "Why didn't I think of it before? … Lizzy! Do you want a part in my movie?"

"Wow!" she yelled, jumping off her horse …

The next thing she knew she was dressed in the costume of Sita, riding hell-for-leather down forest tracks for the cameras. It was hard, repetitive work which she did well, and was much praised and appreciated. She felt a bit bad about Ravi. Not only was Shankar fascinated by her family, but now she had a ride-on part in his father's film too.

"I wish you'd come out riding with me," Lizzy pleaded when she stopped to pick up Ravi on her way to dinner. "It's a lot of fun—you'd love it!"

"You know I don't like horses," Ravi replied, unwillingly tearing his gaze away from his laptop.

"You'd get to see this fantastic forest and all the wildlife instead of burying your head in your computer," Lizzy continued, "You might just as well have stayed in England, you know!"

Insects swarmed around the light outside his tent as they walked out and along the earth pathway to the dining tent.

The warm night pulsed with the sound of crickets as they sat down, and Shankar started quizzing her again about George Abercrombie.

"His character is becoming increasingly important in my book," he explained, and Lizzy was keen to help him as much as possible by searching her memory for every scrap of information. As usual Sunila scribbled down everything.

"Are these lions that Uncle George saved going to be in your book, too?" Lizzy asked.

"I haven't decided yet," Shankar replied. "Even though it's our national symbol, people don't really associate India with lions ... "

"That's true—I thought they only lived in Africa."

"The ones here in the Gir are the last remaining examples of the Asiatic lion which used to be found all the way from Greece to the Ganges. They look very similar to their African cousins but they are more shy."

"Are they dangerous?" Lizzy asked. Vijay hadn't seemed the slightest bit concerned about them when they rode out together—not that they'd seen any ...

"In general, no," Shankar replied, "but sometimes the females will charge to protect their young. If a lioness charges, the best thing to do is to face her and just stand still. She'll lose interest, whereas running away will only excite her more."

Easier said than done! Lizzy thought.

Sitting next to her, Ravi was looking a bit left out of the conversation.

"You should come with me and get a picture of a lion, Ravi," Lizzy told him cheerfully. The only time Ravi came

161

out his tent was when he wanted to take photographs. He took hundreds of shots which he downloaded onto his laptop.

"They're very difficult to photograph," Shankar said. "I've never even seen one of them myself."

Ravi looked at Shankar. He would like to do something to get his attention—all he seemed interested in was Lizzy and her uncle George …

"Okay I'll come out with you, Lizzy," he responded finally.

"Great!" Lizzy beamed.

31

A NARROW ESCAPE

WHEN VIJAY HEARD that Lizzy was intending to take Ravi for a gentle ride on the familiar trails nearby, he saw no reason to accompany them. "Go and come!" he said with a cheerful smile as he waved them off.

Lizzy led the way down the track towards the river. Although she didn't say so, looking at Ravi's white knuckles gripping the reins she realised that it wasn't that he didn't like horses—in fact, he was terrified of them.

Women were washing their clothes in the clear water. Beds of reeds lined the river's edges, and swarms of dragonflies hovered in the air like helicopters. A white-painted shrine peeped out from amongst the trees on the far bank. Lizzy sighed contentedly—the India of the Shalimar murals still existed.

"There are crocodiles in the river further up," Lizzy remarked casually, turning to look at Ravi. He still had an expression of fierce concentration on his face. "Are you doing all right, chuck?" she added in her broadest Yorkshire.

"Fine," he responded between gritted teeth. He wasn't in the mood for jokes.

They followed a track into the forest of teak trees, their dinner-plate-sized green leaves rustling in the warm breeze.

Parrots fluttered through the air and a peacock picked its way across the forest floor, dragging its great tail behind.

There was a commotion in a great banyan tree nearby.

"W … what's that?" Ravi stammered, startled by the noise.

"Stay calm. You'll make the horse nervous. Think yoga breathing."

A group of long-tailed monkeys swung from branch to branch of the banyan, crashing through the foliage, screeching and gibbering angrily.

Lizzy and Ravi watched enthralled, then rode on. Ravi was starting to enjoy himself.

The trail followed a stream up a gorge and they emerged into the foothills of a rocky mountain range. A large lake stretched towards the horizon, buffalo lazing in the shallows with white birds standing on their backs.

"Vijay told me this is a Jain shrine," Lizzy said, pointing to a small temple which stood under a shady tree. Two red-and-white flags fluttered in the warm breeze.

They dismounted, tethered the horses and Ravi wandered down to the lakeside clicking away madly while Lizzy lolled against the shrine. Like her mother, she thought cameras were just a distraction from looking at things properly. She closed her eyes in the sunshine and dozed off …

Waking a few minutes later, she saw Ravi a little way off at the bottom of a boulder-strewn slope. He was crouching down—probably photographing an insect in close-up, Lizzy thought. Suddenly she froze—a huge lioness and two cubs were frolicking in the shade under a tree near him …

Ravi was focused on a termite mound, oblivious to the danger.

"Just stand still!" Lizzy hissed from behind a rocky outcrop.

Ravi stopped dead in his tracks, seeing the crouching lioness.

"I've brought the horses," Lizzy whispered. "Just edge very slowly over to me."

His teeth chattering, never taking his eye off the lioness, Ravi shuffled sideways until he joined Lizzy behind the rocks. They jumped on their horses, Lizzy kicking hers straight away into gallop. Ravi's followed automatically, and he hung on as best he could as they thundered across the dry plain, putting as much distance between the lioness and them as possible.

After what seemed to Ravi like an eternity Lizzy halted her horse. Pushing a dark strand of hair from her brow, she turned to Ravi and grinned. "I hope you got a photo!"

"I think I dropped my camera."

"Do you want to go back and get it? … "

"NO I DO NOT!" Ravi exclaimed, panicking. Sometimes Lizzy had the most preposterous ideas …

"Joking … "

"It's not funny," he grumbled.

"I'm glad we got away at least. I didn't fancy watching you being eaten alive."

Ravi looked at her. "Thanks, Lizzy," he said finally.

"Anytime … " Lizzy peered around her. "Now the question is … where are we?"

32

THE CAVE

THEY WERE LOST. Very lost.

Thunder echoed around the cliffs, making the horses nervous. They'd ridden up a track which Lizzy had thought she recognised, but it had just taken them higher and higher into the mountains.

Way above them they could see a monastery perched on a cliff edge, but it would have taken all day to get there and ask for help.

Ravi fiddled with his mobile. "No signal," he said, shrugging.

There was flash of lightning and the skies opened. They were quickly soaked to the skin.

Ravi spotted the cave first. A flight of stone steps ran up the side of a cliff wall, and at the top was the entrance. "We could shelter up there … " he suggested.

"Yes, and we could leave the horses in here," Lizzy added, leading them into an abandoned cattle pen made of stout thorn bushes. "It must have been made to keep out lions."

They dragged a bush across the opening, and carefully made their way up the decrepit steps. One slip would have sent them plummeting down the cliff face. The cave opening was much bigger than it looked from down below, and they explored further inside. A white-painted, coffin-shaped shrine bedecked with flags sat near the entrance. People had left offerings—garlands of flowers, food and drink.

"Must be some sort of saint," Ravi whispered as they walked in the half-light into the crumbling ruins of an ancient temple. Bats squeaked and swooped in the cave high above them, and the wide stone staircase was sticky with their droppings. The light of the entrance seemed to have shrunk to almost nothing when they reached the rear of the cave and spotted another opening. Stepping through into the next cave, they gasped in awe. A shaft of light poured down from a hole in the roof hundreds of feet above illuminating a stone temple at the bottom of a steep slope. It was covered in intricate sculptures all showing the same benign, smiling figure of a robed man surrounded by worshippers.

"The Lord Buddha!" a voice boomed out of the darkness, and they jumped out of their skins.

An old man with a red-dyed beard and an embroidered cap emerged with a torch in his hand. He didn't seem surprised to see them. "Inside this cave there used to be a Buddhist monastery," he told them in perfect English as he let the torch light play on the marvellous sculptures. "Built on the orders of his follower, the Emperor Asoka himself. The most enlightened ruler of his or any other time—and I, a Sufi, would be the first to say so. You saw the Emperor's inscriptions on the rock as you came up, of course?"

Lizzy shook her head, and explained how she and Ravi came to be in the cave. It was great relief to find someone who could help them. The old man nodded sagely. "A most fortunate occurrence. These caves are little known, yet

168

you have happened upon them by chance. You will take tea with me, but first, here is my torch. You must visit the meditation chamber. Two thousand years ago men would spend weeks on end in there, sat in the darkness without food or drink. And the sannyasin who is buried in the shrine near the entrance did so too."

Lizzy took the torch and they followed in the direction he indicated. They scrambled up a short slope into a narrow tunnel; at the end was a smooth, round boulder half-buried in the sandy floor of the cave.

Lizzy flicked off the torch.

"Hey!" Ravi exclaimed.

"You heard what the old man said … they meditated in total darkness!"

Lizzy sat cross-legged listening to the profound silence. It made no difference to the overwhelming blackness if she kept her eyes open or shut. Random thoughts flitted through her mind, then evaporated.

"What is a sannyasin, anyway?" Lizzy asked eventually.

"Someone who has renounced the world, and lives as a hermit or holy man," Ravi replied. "They exist in all the great Indian religions. They spend their time wandering alone or in remote caves like this, surviving on gifts of food and clothing. You have to be very brave to be a sannyasin."

"You have to be brave to be anything in life."

"That's true," Ravi replied reflectively. "Lizzy, about my riding … it's not that I didn't like horses—"

"I know," Lizzy interrupted gently. "But you've seen off a lioness, so what's a harmless old horse to you?"

"Could you imagine giving everything up to come and live here?" Ravi asked after a few minutes.

"It'd be like running away from home," Lizzy replied. "Except you'd be running away from just about the whole planet. You'd have to be really desperate."

She turned the torch on again, and they made their way back to the entrance to the cave where the old man, who introduced himself as Shah Mustaq Ali, had prepared sweet milky tea on a small fire. Lizzy thought it was the most delicious cuppa she had ever tasted.

They sat together clutching their steaming bowls, the warm sunshine drying their damp clothes as they looked at the view over the craggy ravines.

Lizzy sighed contentedly. She had never felt so completely at peace.

Shah Mustaq Ali broke the silence, pointing towards the white shrine nearby. "This saint lived here over a century ago and had the reputation as the holiest of men, revered by all, yet he was neither Hindu, nor Muslim, nor Jain. Perhaps the most religious thing is to have no religion at all."

"But I thought you said you were a Sufi?" Lizzy asked, thinking of Peregrine.

The old man smiled. "Sufis are mystical Muslims. All religions have their mystical branches, and at that level the differences between them dissolve."

"My Uncle Peregrine is a Sufi," Lizzy said.

Shah Mustaq Ali looked at her curiously. "And what sort of man is he?"

"My Mum thought he was wonderful, but I think he's a bit scary as well."

Shah Mustaq Ali threw his head back and laughed. "Wonderful and scary? Like life itself … "

He was still chuckling to himself as they gathered their things together and made their way back down the steps to the horses. Shah Mustaq Ali had explained that he came from the town of Barvela at the foot of the mountain, and he had promised to show them the way there. While they led the horses down the rugged track Lizzy told him about Uncle George and his involvement in the area.

"I know a little about George Abercrombie from my studies of our history, but my friend the Raja of Barvela knows far more … " He hesitated a moment, a look of concern in his kind eyes. Then he seemed to make up his mind. "I will take you to his palace and introduce you."

His palace! Lizzy imagined it would be like the Taj Mahal hotel. Perhaps the Raja would have elephants they could ride on …

33

THE PALACE OF BARVELA

IT WAS LATE AFTERNOON by the time they led the horses into the small sleepy town of Barvela. A bullock ambled down the road pulling a cart overflowing with fresh-cut sugar cane, and a flea-bitten mongrel dozed in the sun, its tail flicking idly in the dust. At the centre of the town Shah Mustaq Ali ushered them through a wooden gateway in a high mud wall. They approached a mildew-stained concrete bungalow from the 1920s set in an unkempt garden.

A man in tatty Indian clothes appeared from around the back of the house and at a word from Shah Mustaq Ali took the horses from them and led them away.

Shah Mustaq Ali told Lizzy and Ravi to wait a moment in the porch and went inside. Lizzy assumed they were stopping at his house to pick up something before going on to the palace, and was surprised when he reappeared with a fat, moustachioed man wearing a stained cricket sweater.

"Well, well! A descendant of George Abercrombie in Barvela after all these years," the man greeted them in perfect old-fashioned English, eyeing Lizzy askance. "Even so, I suppose I must bid you welcome." He shook their hands, leading them into the house. He shouted into the gloom for someone to bring tea and ushered them into an internal courtyard with peeling pink painted walls and rickety cane chairs.

"Please sit!" he said. "You must let your father know you are here, young man!" he insisted as a scruffy servant arrived with tea. "From what Shah Mustaq Ali tells me he must be worried about you!"

"Here?" said Ravi doubtfully, checking that his mobile was getting a signal. "Where shall I say 'here' is?"

"The palace, of course! The driver will need only ask in the town and he'll be directed!"

Ravi looked almost as astonished as Lizzy felt. If this mouldering house was the palace, then their host must be ...

"The Raja has something very particular he wants to tell you," Shah Mustaq Ali murmured to Lizzy confidentially, as Ravi went into the open courtyard to make his call. "Although it's not easy for him, even now ... "

"Oh!" Lizzy said, mystified. The Raja was looking coolly at her.

"My friend tells me you're Abercrombie's great-great-great granddaughter, no?" the Raja said. Lizzy nodded. "Well, I suppose he had to be found out sometime."

Found out? Lizzy thought, feeling uncomfortable "Found out for what?" she said.

"We must wait for your young friend, mustn't we?" he continued, signalling to his servant to pour the tea as Ravi talked to KK. "Everything out in the open. Our families should have no secrets. Not any more."

He sat back in his chair calmly drinking his tea as Lizzy's mind whirred, wondering what he could possibly mean.

"There'll be someone over in an hour or so," Ravi said as he rejoined them. "Apparently Vijay hadn't even told Dad that we were missing. He was livid with him."

Lizzy came down to earth with a bump. She hoped Vijay wouldn't get into too much trouble—he'd been very nice to her.

"Come!"

The Raja stood up unexpectedly, beckoning them to follow him through into the small, high-ceilinged living room. It was full to the brim with enormous pieces of dilapidated furniture, a stuffed leopard and other moth-eaten hunting trophies. Vast portraits of magnificently dressed Rajas and Ranis were hung on the stained, peeling wallpaper.

"All this stuff comes from my family's old palace—long gone, sadly," the Raja explained, gesturing expressively. "It's all much too big for here, as you see, but I can't find it in my heart to throw away my history." He talked vaguely about one or two of the people in the paintings, then paused in front of a small portrait of a beautiful young woman with delicate features and fine, dark eyes. His expression clouded over.

"This is Leela," he told them, "My great-great-grandmother's sister. Her marriage was engineered for political advantage by the Regent of Junagadh more than a hundred years ago. But her husband abandoned her, taking with him Krishna, their young son—and then married another woman. Leela died by her own hand when she heard. It was a tragedy my family has never forgotten."

"How sad," Lizzy murmured sympathetically.

"Yes, indeed," the Raja said, turning to look at her. "How sad, as you say. But then what do you expect if you marry a Britisher? Her husband's name was George Abercrombie."

Lizzy felt as if she'd been kicked in the stomach. "M ... m ... my Uncle G ... George?" she stammered, astonished. "B ... b ... but I had no idea!"

"How could you have known?" the Raja replied. "He would hardly have told his English wife, would he? The whole thing was a secret known only by my family and the Nawabs. He even converted to Hinduism to marry her. If the British had found out it would have ruined his career."

"But if he married Penelope when he was already married to Leela ... " Lizzy reflected, frowning. "That would make him—"

"A bigamist. Not a crime in our world, then, but in yours ... " The Raja shrugged.

"But Lizzy," Ravi cut in, "You told me that when George disappeared, Penelope was still alive. So he may have ... "

"Abandoned her too, you mean?" Lizzy said slowly as the possibility dawned on her.

"What's this?" the Raja asked, cottoning on. "He did the same thing to his English wife, you say. The scoundrel!" Lizzy shook her head. That her Uncle George, her favourite ancestor, should be so ... so ...

"You said he had a son by Leela?" Shah Mustaq Ali asked the Raja. "What happened to him?"

"Apparently he took Krishna to England to put him into boarding school—as they did in those days," he explained. "George Abercrombie was supposed to come back and take up a post as Resident of Lucknow—a very grand position indeed. Leela waited and waited—and then his successor showed her an announcement he'd seen in *The Times* at his Mumbai club—George had married and settled in England. She was devastated."

"So what happened to the boy in England?" asked Shah Mustaq Ali, looking at Lizzy, who shrugged, dumbstruck. This was all too much to take in at once.

But the Raja hadn't finished yet. He went over to the huge heavy mahogany bookcase that took up most of one wall, and opened one of the glass-fronted doors exposing stacks of dusty leather-bound volumes.

"When George Abercrombie and Leela lived together in Junagadh," he told them as he put on his reading glasses and searched through the books, "they had a servant who stayed faithful to her when she was abandoned and moved back to Barvela. Years after she had died this servant gave a book to the Raja of the time ... now where is it?" He blew the dust off a couple of books. "No ... Ah! Here we are!"

He turned and looked at Lizzy, holding in front of him a small book held together with a brass clasp. The brown-leather binding had turned a mottled yellow with age and damp. The Raja looked kindly at Lizzy for the first time.

"I see I have shocked you, Miss Abercrombie, and may have trampled on your finer feelings. You must forgive me; the faults of your ancestor are no fault of yours. But so many generations of my own forbears were lectured on the way they chose to live their lives by you high-minded British that you should know that they, too, had feet of clay." He put the book down on a table. "If you will accept this from me, I would like to think this may be some sort of recompense. Maybe you will be able to read what my tired old eyes cannot."

He opened the book and signalled for Lizzy to come forwards. She looked down, and read the capital letters handwritten neatly in faded black ink:

THE JOURNAL OF GEO. ABERCROMBIE

Her hand trembling, she turned through the pages; they were all covered in an untidy, crabbed writing, virtually illegible. She came across a folded piece of yellowed paper sandwiched between the pages on which was written '*Leela*'.

She opened it breathlessly; inside was a thick lock of jet-black hair. Replacing it carefully, she leafed through to the end, and her heart skipped a beat. Across the last page was scrawled in large letters …

MOONSTONE

… the *O*'s overlapping, one light and one dark. Like the moon eclipsing the sun.

34

DEPARTURES AND ARRIVALS

L IZZY WAS TRYING TO TELL Johnny Cairo all about their adventures in Gujarat but Kiran kept interrupting, asking Johnny if he knew so-and-so, what's-is-name and whojamaflip, all famous film stars in LA whom she claimed were her best friends.

She really is a pain, Lizzy thought, as Ravi's beautiful cousin monopolised the conversation. She was pleased to see that Johnny didn't seem to notice Kiran's endless legs and perfect almond eyes.

At the other end of the dining table Kitten was squeezing every last detail of the lion story from Ravi, Oh-my-God-ing every other second. She'd invited Kiran and Johnny to join them for dinner before they left on the night flight back to London.

The bearer came in and told Kitten that the car was ready to take them to the airport.

"Lizzy! Ravi!" she said, clapping her hands. "Chop, chop! Time to go!"

Back in her room, Lizzy quickly checked to see that she'd left nothing behind. She carefully wrapped the journal in layers of newspaper and put it in the middle of her clothes in her suitcase to protect it. Satisfied, she wheeled the case through to the hallway where everyone was waiting amid the pile of luggage to say their goodbyes. Kiran was droning on and on to Johnny about Mumbai shopping malls and how they were " … so like not even last season. Eouw!"

Johnny told Lizzy he'd stay in touch, and Kiran gave him her email address, insisting that he get in touch next time he was in California.

There was a ring at the doorbell of the penthouse.

"Who on earth can that be?" Kitten said, glancing at her watch.

The bearer opened the door and in walked Shankar, looking as lean and distinguished as ever.

"Oh my God!" Kitten cried, embracing him. " Wonderful! I thought you said you were in Ahmedebad! But we're just going … !"

"I tried to get here in time to have dinner with you all, but the traffic is appalling!" he said. "But at least I get to say to say goodbye." He turned to Lizzy and smiled. "I hear you had an interesting time in Barvela. Kitten told me all about George and his Indian wife."

"I was totally gobsmacked," Lizzy said. "I still am, as a matter of fact. I can hardly believe it. They even had a son I've never heard of."

"I understand, but it's much less shocking than you'd think," Shankar replied. "When the British first came to India in the sixteen hundreds, many of them took Indian wives or girlfriends, and even passed them onto their friends when they finally went home. But by George's time it wasn't the done thing at all. It would certainly have destroyed his chances of promotion if it had been known."

"That's the strange thing," Lizzy said. "It must have been a real love match for him to risk so much. So something

180

really dramatic must have happened to make him leave her. But I'm sure I'll find out when I manage to read the journal… "

"It's such a shame she hasn't time to show you it, Shankar," said Kitten, checking her watch anxiously. "He even kept a lock of the Princess's hair in it! So romantic!" She signalled for the bearers to start loading the luggage into the lift.

"I'll send you a copy when I've deciphered the hand-writing, " Lizzy said.

"We really must be going … " Kitten said, ushering everyone out. "I'm so sorry, Shankar. Stay here a while—Ramesh will give you something to eat, at least."

"Deciphered?" Shankar asked, following Lizzy out onto the landing as she got into the lift.

"Yes, the handwriting is really difficult to make out," she told him as they all crammed in. "But I could read one word, in odd big writing at the end … Moonstone. Does it mean anything to you?"

"No," Shankar said with a shrug. "Most intriguing … "

The lift doors slid shut.

Shankar wasn't the slightest bit hungry. He walked out onto the terrace and looked from high down onto the whole seething city, lights stretching to the far horizon, traffic snaking through high-rise canyons and shanty slums, boats ploughing the dark waters. He lit a cigarette and asked Ramesh to bring him a *peg* of Scotch. Reaching into the pocket of his linen suit, he took out the old clasp knife which he carried with him everywhere. He breathed on the tarnished silver handle, and polished it with his handkerchief—and for the thousandth time read the inscription.

"This is taking for ever!" Lizzy fumed.

They were waiting by the baggage carousel at Heathrow Airport. Kitten was standing to the back of the crowd, shouting instructions to Ravi who kept responding impatiently that the bags from their flight were only just starting to come through.

His mobile phone rang, and his eyes widened in surprise when he heard who it was at the other end.

"Ravi!" Shankar's voice sounded urgent—secretive almost. "Have you passed through immigration?"

"Yes, but … "

"Don't say my name out loud, and move away from Lizzy and your mother! There's something I must tell you."

Ravi did as he was told automatically. He'd never received a call from Shankar before.

"Has the luggage arrived yet?"

"It's just starting to come through … "

" Listen very carefully to what I say. There is something in that journal which is potentially extremely dangerous to Lizzy. It's to do with the Moonstone. Here's what you must do … "

A minute later, Ravi rejoined Lizzy by the side of the carousel. "Why don't you keep my Mum company, Lizzy?" he suggested. "I know what your bags look like."

"I'd rather stay here … "

"Mum hates to be alone," Ravi continued, "and I can't go."

"Okay" Lizzy agreed reluctantly. She didn't want to miss her suitcases, especially the one with the journal.

Half-an-hour later it had still failed to appear even though all their other bags were stacked up on the trolley. Her mobile rang.

"Dad!" she exclaimed. "Where are you?"

Her father was waiting at the other side of customs and was worried about the delay because they had the long drive up to Yorkshire ahead of them. Lizzy was explaining about the missing case and the journal when Kitten interrupted …

"Hello, Henry?" she purred warmly when she took the phone from Lizzy. "How are you? Look, don't worry about the case, Ravi and I will sort it out and have it sent on. We've only got to get to central London—you've got miles to go … I'll send Lizzy out, okay?"

"There, that's agreed," she told Lizzy after she'd finished. "You go through to your father and we'll deal with the case. He's looking forward so much to seeing you."

Lizzy gave in, and was soon reunited with her father who looked better than he had done for ages and hugged her warmly—something he rarely did.

As they headed around the M25 she told him what she had found out about Uncle George. He was astonished to hear about his earlier marriage, and most interested in the son that he had brought to England with him.

"That means we may have relatives here that we have no idea about. Imagine! Did the Raja tell you the boy's name?"

"Krishna, I think he said … "

"It's unlikely he'd have kept a name like that. It's going to be difficult find out what happened to him."

183

"Maybe the journal will help … " As Lizzy told her father about it, her mobile rang.

"I've just found your case!" Ravi reassured her. "It was behind a pillar—someone must have taken it mistakenly and just left it there."

"Brilliant!" said Lizzy. "Listen, why not bring it to school with you on Thursday? I don't want it going missing again … "

"No problem—that's what I was going to suggest anyway. Give my regards to your father."

"I will. And Ravi?"

"Yeah?"

"Thanks for everything. I had a great time."

"So did I. See you at school." Ravi put the phone down and sighed with relief. He'd managed to do what Shankar wanted without a hitch.

As they drove up the A1 towards Yorkshire, they talked more about Uncle George. Later, when she started telling him about her own adventures, he listened with polite interest, but he seemed miles away in his own dreamland.

There was a pause in the conversation and he cleared his throat, glancing at Lizzy.

"Rose is coming to dinner tonight," he told her. "Actually, I've seen quite a bit of her while you've been away."

35

BACK AT SCHOOL

WHEN RAVI HAD BROUGHT her bag back to school with him as planned, Lizzy couldn't wait to get working on the journal. But then she surprised him in his study later that day, finding him with a scan of the journal on the screen of his computer.

"What do you think you're doing!" she said.

"I thought you would be pleased," he protested. "You nearly lost the journal once already."

"So you opened my luggage and scanned my Uncle George's journal, and then put it back so I would think nothing had happened? What's going on?"

"All right, all right, I'll get rid of them then," Ravi said, but he was so flustered as Lizzy glared over his shoulder while he tried to close down the pages, that he hit the wrong key and a draft of an email he was about to send popped up.

"What the ... !" Lizzy shouted, pulling Ravi's hands from the keys. "*Dear Shankar,*" she read, "*Here are the scans of the journal as promised. Please,* please, *let me know if there is anything I can do to keep Lizzy out of danger ...* "

"What the hell is this?" Lizzy said, her dark eyes flashing furiously.

"Sh ... Sh ... Shankar told me that there might be something in the journal about the M ... M ... Moonstone which could be harmful to you," Ravi stammered. "He insisted I should scan it—otherwise something terrible might happen ... "

"That's ridiculous! Shankar said he didn't know anything about the Moonstone!"

"Did he?" Ravi looked confused.

"What sort danger anyhow? Why didn't he come straight out with it?"

"I dunno," Ravi said "He seemed so serious, I just did what I was told."

"He lied so effortlessly," Lizzy mused. "And in any case, I'd already offered to send him a copy ... "

"He must have wanted to find out something before you did," Ravi said, desperate to be helpful. "I'm really sorry, Lizzy, but I did think ... "

"I don't like this at all! He's up to something!"

Lizzy looked at the computer screen, and idea struck her.

"Show me one of the scans," she said.

Ravi eagerly complied.

"High resolution?" she asked.

"Of course," he said. "It's hard enough to read as it is."

"What does the same page look like in low res?"

Ravi tapped away quickly at the keys. "There!" he said after a moment. Lizzy carefully inspected the two scans, and smiled.

"Okay, Mr Shankar Pujari, game on! You can have your scans. Here's what we're going to do, Ravi. And if you play your cards right, I may even forgive you being such a jerk."

From that moment Lizzy set to work deciphering Uncle George's journal. It was no easy task. She borrowed a magnifying glass on a stand and found a secluded corner of the library where she could set up her laptop to work undisturbed. Each word of the spidery handwriting took quite some time to unravel, then she typed it into the computer and tackled the next one.

It was nearly bedtime when Lizzy reached the end of the first paragraph, and the final word made her feel sick to the pit of her stomach.

It was the old sannyasin who made me realise the full enormity of what I had done. In a moment of madness I had stolen the Moonstone, and by another calamitous act I was prevented from ever returning it. I thanked God that I had no children, so at least there were to be no future generations at Shalimar whose lives would be blighted by its terrible curse.

Lizzy tossed and turned all that night. The mention of the curse brought all the memories of her mother's death flooding back … her blood … the Moonstone … the full moon …

In the first light of morning she went back to the library And for four long weeks Lizzy became like a hermit. She went through lessons on auto-pilot: her every spare moment was spent deciphering the journal.

When she had finally finished she printed it out in its entirety. It was only then that she realised how drained and exhausted she felt. She needed a break, a distraction … She put the printout into her rucksack, and wandered out of the library and across the school grounds to the riding stables. Spring had given way to summer without her even noticing—it was a beautiful evening, but the neatly mown lawns were strangely deserted.

Unlike the riding school. Lizzy looked down from the stand into the packed arena.

It seemed as if half Laythorpe College was there—even Ravi, learning in his methodical way how make a horse go from trot to canter and back again. The Sams seethed with indignation as they were forced into a far corner on Stetson and Hardy—they used to having the run of the place and now there was hardly room for them to practise their jumping.

"If it isn't our school movie star. Where've you been hidin' yerself?"

Lizzy turned to find Alison Studley standing behind her with an amused expression on her face.

"What's going on?" Lizzy asked.

"It's all your fault—you've made it right trendy, Lizzy," Alison complained good-humouredly. "The school's had to hire a couple of new assistant instructors. I reckon they should send the bill to you … "

"What?" Lizzy said, puzzled.

The news had spread like wildfire round Laythorpe College that she had a ride-on part in *The Lifeline*, Alison told her, and everyone wanted to learn to ride like her.

Lizzy was amazed. It was as if she had been living on a different planet.

"So where've you been?" Alison asked again.

"Busy," Lizzy replied vaguely. "I've had lots of work to do."

And unfortunately she hadn't finished yet. With a sigh she made her way to her favourite bench by an old brick wall overgrown with tangled roses. She took out the journal, and started to read.

The first pages were about Uncle George's early life and his childhood sweetheart, Penelope, whom he wasn't allowed to marry unless he made his fortune. So he decided to go to India to seek it …

I left on the East Indiaman Walmer Castle *after begging Penelope to keep herself for me—just you see, said I, I'll be back with a fortune that will impress even your father before you know what. Then followed tears, vows and promises to write every week, no, every day—everything you'd expect from two star-crossed lovers. To give the lass credit, she kept much closer to her side of the bargain than I did to mine: in the end, it was I who let her down by falling in love with someone else.*

It takes a particular kind of man to really prosper out East, and I wasn't the kind. To be sure, I worked fit to drop and cultivated what I thought were the right sort of friends and steadily rose through the ranks. Steady. That became my defining feature: send Abercrombie, he's a steady man. So I was posted where a firm hand was required, but not too firm, or to a district where the appearance of even-handedness in a delicate negotiation was all-important. Steady Abercrombie, he'd never do anything unpredictable. Little did they know.

You see, by this time, the East India Company was reaching the end of its rule in India and had changed beyond recognition. The traders and merchants—one step away from pirates, most of them—that the Company had first sent there two hundred years ago had given way to soldiers and administrators. God-fearing folk to a man, they liked to think they were in the business of looking after the Indians, rather like a schoolmaster looks after his pupils—words of encouragement to the good little boys, the big stick for those who stepped out of line. Hypocritical tosh, of course—we were there because we'd conquered it, and India provided England with a comfortable living for relatively little effort. But it was true that gone were the days of

189

wild opportunity where a king's ransom could be laid at your feet if
you played your cards right, and the Devil take the hindmost. What
was now needed was reliability, honesty and a sense of duty. So
you'd think my reputation for steadiness would serve me well, and
to an extent it did. Except that my regular letters from Penelope kept
reminding me why I was really there—I didn't want to be steady, I
wanted to be rich.

But then George had fallen in love with Leela, an Indian
princess. They had been able to keep the marriage secret
from the British authorities with the collusion of the rulers
of Junagadh and the help of her family—even after they'd
had a son, Krishna. But when he was promoted to become
Resident of Lucknow, he couldn't refuse without attracting
attention. Nor could he figure out how would be able to
afford to keep his family in secret there …

While I was pondering these financial problems I went to Veraval
to meet a company of troops from Bombay on their way to Rajkot.
Arriving before their ship, I decided to visit the celebrated Temple of
the Moon at Somnath. I had heard rumours about the Moonstone,
the fabulous diamond that was fixed in the forehead of the idol of
the Moon God, and the temple itself was supposed to be one of the
most sacred in all India.

At the very moment when I was about to walk into the temple the
whole area was shaken by the most tremendous earthquake, causing
wide scale destruction and huge loss of life. Luckily I was in the
courtyard, but from inside the ruined temple I could hear the screams
of survivors. I picked my way through the collapsed columns to
see if I could rescue anyone. From under a heap of rubble a dark
arm projected, and grabbing the hand, I tugged. It was no shattered
human frame that I pulled clear, but the idol of the Moon God,

the Moonstone gleaming eerily in its forehead! Without a moment's hesitation I took my clasp knife and gouged out the diamond and, ignoring the moans of the injured, left the temple, mounted my horse and rode to Veraval. Not one person had witnessed my actions in that evil hour.

From that moment my life became one of scheming and deception. I had the means to solve my financial problems, but it would by no means be straightforward—the Moonstone was famed throughout India for a particular flaw it possessed, and I couldn't sell it without detection. I had home leave due to me before taking up the Lucknow appointment, and with Leela's agreement I took Krishna to England with me to put him into school there, as was the custom then even for Company officials with relatively little money to spare. My plan was to go to Antwerp and have the Moonstone cut into smaller diamonds before selling them. In any case the diamond's flaw undermined its value and it would be better cut out. This flaw was the most strange thing; the diamond was afire with light from every angle—except one, where it was as if the light was sucked into the stone, and it turned black. This was why the Moonstone was considered sacred in India—like the sun and the moon, it had the properties of both light and dark. I took no notice of such things, but neither did I then know about the curse.

After the long voyage home around the Cape I stayed at my London club, the Oriental, making the arrangements for Krishna—whom I had renamed Christopher Jones—and contemplating my trip to Antwerp. A fellow member known to me from the old days in Yorkshire told me that Penelope had recently come into a considerable fortune upon the death of her father. "Penelope Rawlstone is the toast of London society, and much courted by all the young bucks," my friend told me. I thought no more about her.

Shortly afterwards I received two letters which had come from India by express mail. One was from Mavroleon, who had succeeded me as Resident at Junagadh. He regretfully informed me that Leela had died of cholera. The other was from the Nawab, conveying his condolences. All meaning drained from my life at that moment. For weeks I kept to my room at the club, and then, in my loneliness and despair, I contacted Penelope.

She was overjoyed to see me, and for her at least it was as if my years in India had never been. She chided me about the letter I had written telling her to forget all about me, and was so loving and devoted that had it not been for the memory of Leela I might have fallen for her over again. That was beyond the means of my broken heart, but, I reasoned, with all prospect of my own happiness destroyed, perhaps at least I could make Penelope content. Despite many rivals, I persuaded her to marry me.

Having married her fortune, I threw in my career in India, and settled down to life as a Yorkshire country gentleman. Penelope encouraged me to rebuild the house she'd inherited and I chose to do so in the Indian style. Little did she suspect that it was a memorial to my lost love, Leela, or that I renamed it Shalimar to recall our first meeting.

Of course, I no longer needed to sell the Moonstone. By this time it had started to make its baleful influence felt—it haunted me as a recurrent nightmare haunts a dreamer. Many was the time I simply wanted to throw it away, to be rid of it, but I could not find the courage, and instead would find myself gazing at it for hours on end. The stone's elusive flaw became my obsession; sometimes it was impossible to find, at others it was hard to avoid.

I started to spend more and more time in the library of the Oriental, studying the tellurian and searching rare books for references to the Moonstone. The loss of the stone was well known to some members of the club, and one way or another I learnt of the curse. It was said that anyone who stole the Moonstone from its rightful place would live and die miserably. I cast my mind back to when I first took the stone and realised that from that moment my troubles had begun. Its theft had led me to separate from Leela and so I was unable to comfort her in her illness or to prevent her death. My marriage to Penelope, although comfortable, was loveless and barren. Was I perhaps cursed by the Moonstone?

The idea of a curse seemed outlandish, but I couldn't get it out of my mind. In my folly, I thought I could defeat it with science. How many hours did I spend making notes in Colonel Hunt's The Chronology of Creation, *devising a way to defeat the curse of the stone? The astronomical calculations contained in that worthy volume spurred me on. Eventually, fool that I was, I thought I had the answer, and created a special place in the old priest's hole at Shalimar where the stone could be safely hidden and yet subjected to the influence I had designed for it. I had determined that if the Moonstone was exposed to the light of the full moon on the summer solstice—a moment of rare cosmic harmony occurring only once every thirty years—then it would be rebalanced and the curse neutralised. I predicted that the moonbeam at that moment would cause the diamond to light up with unequalled brilliance. If only I had spent as much time and energy getting the Moonstone back to Somnath as I spent 'rebalancing' it … but our greed and stupidity blinds us to the obvious often enough.*

Lizzy put the papers down on the bench, and breathed deeply. The curse that had killed her mother was caused by the Moonstone, and the sacred diamond was still hidden at Shalimar, in the old priest's hole …

36

FRUSTRATION

"WHAT DO YOU MEAN, it'll take a few more weeks to finish!" Shankar shouted down the phone in the study of his house in Los Angeles. "I've paid you a *lakh* rupees already, more than you'd normally earn in five years, and all you've come up with so far is a reference to some obscure book in a library in London … "

He listened impatiently while the man on the other end of the phone in India tried to explain.

"If only I had better scans, sahib," Shankar imitated his whining voice mercilessly. "Well you can't have better scans, I've already told you that. You're the specialist, do your job!"

He slammed the phone down, furious that Ravi had made such a bodge of scanning the journal, and furious that it was too late do anything about it now.

He flopped down in a leather armchair and poured himself a large whisky. He'd thought he was so near to his goal when he'd first heard about the journal, but the manuscript expert from the Prince of Wales museum he'd bribed to transcribe the scans had worked so agonisingly slowly …

He took a great gulp from the glass. Keep calm, he told himself. You haven't spent a lifetime searching for the Moonstone just to blow it when at last the end is in sight. He remembered how as a young Brahmin at the Temple of the Moon he'd first been told the history of the Moonstone—how some said the diamond was the legendary Symantaka told of in the *Vishnu Purana*, a gift of the Sun God himself; how it had been honoured in the Temple since time immemorial; how it had been pillaged by the marauding Mohammed of Ghazni in 1024 and how, from that time, it had passed through the bloodied hands of successive tyrants, adventurers and princes until finally it had been recovered by his ancestors and, in a secret ceremony that drew Brahmins from all over India, restored to the idol of the Moon God in 1848. Holy men had marvelled at it, scientists had measured and studied it, metaphysicians had pondered the nature of its elusive flaw. And then he had learnt how the Moonstone had miraculously survived the great earthquake that had destroyed the Temple in 1858, dug from the rubble months later by his own great-great grandfather, one of the few surviving Brahmins there.

But when Shankar was researching his college thesis on the sacred diamonds of India he had happened upon the sales ledger of Edgar & Sons, a long defunct Mumbai jeweler. And there, dated a few weeks after the earthquake was noted 'Glass Replica based on drawings supplied by the customer, Mr Rajendra Pujari. Sold, one thousand rupees." With startling clarity, the realisation came to him that the Moonstone had not been found after the earthquake, and that his ancestor had planted the replica in the rubble, hailing it as the recovered Moonstone in order to ensure that the Temple would be rebuilt—and that the Pujari family would continue to live on the rich pickings from the pilgrims.

As indeed they had done, in blissful ignorance of the fact that the so-called sacred Moonstone in the forehead of the idol was just a glass replica! But when Shankar had tried to convince his brother Brahmins of that, they at first ignored him, accusing him of sacrilege for wanting to examine the Moonstone closely, then telling him he was dangerously obsessed, and when finally they found him breaking into the archives to try to gather more evidence of the the Moonstone's theft, they'd banished him for ever.

Callow youth as he was, he'd vowed that he would dedicate his life to recovering the Moonstone and returning it to the Temple, its rightful place. That would show them, he'd thought! But he came to realise that his former Brahmin bretheren were such hypocrites, they were not worthy of his righteous intentions. So he had decided to make his own way, to make his own mark on the world—while they stayed at the Temple, free dhal and chapattis the limit of their ambitions.

He'd never lost his obsession with the Moonstone, even as he'd grown ever more successful and wealthy. But then fate had another twist in store for him—he'd finally managed to break into the Temple archives, looking for clues, and amongst the documents concerning the diamond had discovered something of such momentous importance that he knew at once how he could harness its sacred power. Harness it for himself.

He took another slug. There was still work to do.

37

A TRIP TO LONDON

"DAD?" Lizzy asked nervously when she rang him from school. She was still reeling from having just finished the whole journal, but she knew there was no time to lose. The solstice was in five weeks' time ...

"Hello, Lizzy," he replied. Rose was sitting at the dining table—they'd just finished supper.

"You know I'm allowed out next weekend?" she continued.

"Yes, of course, I'm picking you up on Saturday morning ... "

"Would you take me to London? You know I haven't been for ages."

"It's very short notice, Lizzy ... " It was already Wednesday night.

"Please, Dad. It would be nice for us to go away together, wouldn't it?"

"Yes, it would," her father agreed. He'd been making a big effort to get closer to Lizzy since Christmas.

"We could stay at your club ... " Lizzy suggested. She made it sound very casual, but in fact that was the only reason she wanted to go.

"I'm not sure the Oriental allows children ... "

"But you could ask, couldn't you?"

"I suppose I could," he conceded. It was years since he had been to the Oriental, his London gentleman's club. His father had inscribed William and him as life members shortly after they were born. It was a family tradition that went all the way back to George Abercrombie.

The next morning Henry called the club and found to his surprise that children were allowed at weekends. He booked two rooms and called Lizzy back straight away.

"I'll take you, Lizzy, but you'll have to dress up a bit. No jeans or trainers."

"That's okay," Lizzy agreed. "Thanks, Dad—it'll be fun, you'll see."

"I'm sure it will. And Lizzy, please remember the journal. I know you say there's nothing interesting in it, but I'd like to see it anyway."

"Yes, Dad," Lizzy assured him, even though she had no intention of bringing it.

Henry was puzzled. It was going to be Lizzy's first visit to London for a long time and yet she seemed much more interested in his club than anything else. She plied him with questions about it all morning as they sped down from York to King's Cross on the train.

His vague answers infuriated Lizzy. Finally, he looked up from his newspaper. "Your mother used to love staying there," he said.

Lizzy felt a sudden pang of intense loneliness. She would have told her mother everything …

"Is there any mention of the club in the journal?" her father asked.

"No," Lizzy answered, pretending to look out of the train window at the late spring landscape rushing by.

"You did bring it with you, didn't you?"

"Oh dear! I'm so sorry, I forgot it … " Lizzy thought of the journal lying locked up in her desk drawer. She didn't mention the printout in her bag.

"Well, never mind," her father shrugged. "The main thing about this weekend is that we're together. We can go to the theatre, the Tower of London, shopping, whatever you like … "

The Oriental was a vast old building taking up a whole corner of Hanover Square. The great entrance hallway was full of Eastern curios—an Egyptian mummy case stood against a wall, a long glistening teak war canoe sat in the middle of the marble floor, and a pair of tall Chinese screens concealed a door. There was an alcove containing a stone sculpture of a four-armed god with an elephant's head, and a huge bronze temple bell hung on an elaborately carved ebony frame over the porter's desk. A wizened old porter in a crumpled dark-blue uniform looked up from his newspaper as they approached.

"Afternoon, Mr Abercrombie," he greeted him in a chirpy Cockney accent. " 'Aven't seen you in town for quite some time, sir."

"Good afternoon, Jack," Henry replied. "You're right, it's been too long. This is my daughter, Lizzy."

Lizzy smiled. "Hello."

"Jack knows everything there is to know about the club," her father told her.

"Too right … " Jack confirmed.

"You must tell me which rooms she's allowed in," Henry continued. "Frankly I was amazed to find that the club lets children in at all."

"I know, sir," Jack grumbled good-humouredly. "First it's women, now it's children. What's the world comin' to, that's what I want to know? You can use the dinin' room, but the library, bar and smokin' room are for adult members only. Like the Turkish baths, of course."

"Where is the library?" Lizzy enquired, adding quickly, " … So I don't go in by mistake."

Jack pointed to the door. "You won't have 'eard about our new member if you ain't been for a while, sir," he told her father conversationally. "That famous Indian writer joined a few days back, didn't 'e just … Mr Shankar Pujari." He turned to Lizzy. "You'll have read his book, Miss, I'm sure."

A shiver ran up Lizzy's spine. What if Shankar had managed to decipher the journal after all, and even now was on the trail?

"Lizzy knows Shankar Pujari very well," Henry told Jack proudly.

"Does she, now?" Jack said, catching sight of a young, well-dressed Chinese man walking briskly past, "Did you hear that, Mr Hao?"

He halted. "I beg your pardon?" Mr Hao asked Jack politely.

"This young lady is a friend of Mr Pujari."

He bowed. "Then I am honoured to meet you," he said, holding out his hand. "I am Deng Hao, the librarian at the club, and Mr Pujari has recently been in contact with me. I would be honoured to meet a friend of his."

"Henry Abercrombie." He shook hands with Mr Hao. "But it is my daughter Lizzy who knows Mr Pujari."

Lizzy wished the ground would swallow her up. The last thing she wanted was for Shankar to know that she had been at the club. "Hello," she said, taking his hand as coolly as politeness allowed.

Mr Hao smiled. "Mr Pujari has been kind enough to say that our library here is what attracted him to the club. He intends to visit at the first opportunity."

I bet he does, thought Lizzy. She was just in the nick of time.

"And may I ask what is your connection with him?" Mr Hao continued.

"Lizzy had a small part in the film of *The Lifeline*," her father explained when she mumbled a reply.

Both Mr Hao and Jack looked at her with interest. *Now Shankar's bound to find out I've been here*, she thought bleakly.

"I am very pleased to have met you," Mr Hao said with a small bow, and walked quickly off in the direction of the library.

Across the hallway a man in loose Indian clothes opened the door to the bar and the sound of uproarious laughter spilled out. Then there was a curious *phhht!* sound and a thud, and ... "Damned good shot, Usman!"

"What's that?" Lizzy asked, anxious to change the subject.

"It's the annual blowpipe darts competition today," Jack explained. "Same as darts," he added, "but you use a blowpipe instead of chucking them." *Phhht!* went the blowpipe again, and another dart thudded unseen into the board. "It was the idea of Raja Brooke. He brought the equipment back from Sarawak in 1856. The feathers on the darts have gorn a bit ragged, but at least the poison has worn off the tips."

As he was talking a tall man with sleek black hair, a large moustache and steady dark eyes came out of a large door decorated with intricate brass work at the other side of the hall, locking it carefully and putting the huge key on the reception desk with a flourish. He looked at Jack expectantly while adjusting the pink rose he wore in the buttonhole of his immaculate white suit.

Jack picked the key up with due ceremony. "Right you are, Ibrahim Pasha, sir." He put the key in a small cupboard—as the door opened Lizzy noticed a discreet label saying 'HAREM' inside—and locked it with a much smaller key, which he handed to Ibrahim Pasha with a bow. He slipped it into his pocket and left.

Jack nodded towards the decorated door. "Installed a hundred years ago for Mehmet Ali, Viceroy of Egypt, that was … came with twenty-three of 'em once … " He was about to tell Lizzy more, but her father put up his hand.

"I'll explain it to her later," he interrupted hurriedly. Just then two of the most massive men Lizzy had ever seen came through the front door. They walked across to the desk. One looked Japanese; the other had ginger whiskers and pale freckly skin. Jack glanced up at them briefly.

"You're in the St James' Room today, gentlemen," he told them. "First floor and follow the signs." Lizzy watched in amazement as they ran nimbly up the grand staircase.

"Sumo wrestlers," Jack explained, following her stare. "Mr McMorran used to toss cabers, but there wasn't much money in it."

He gave them the keys to their rooms and called a young porter over to take their bags. "By the way, the Japanese tea ceremony starts at four this afternoon, sir, if that's of any interest," the porter said as they turned towards the stairs. "But I wouldn't advise it if your goin' to the theatre or anyfink. It goes on 'til eight."

"Thanks, Jack, but I think we'll give that a miss."

Lizzy's mind boggled at the thought of taking four hours to have tea.

After they installed themselves in their bedrooms they spent the rest of the day sightseeing, and then went to the theatre in the evening. It was all great fun, but Lizzy's heart wasn't really in it. She had too much on her mind. Her father said he was exhausted when they got back to the club and climbed the stairs.

"We've got a long day tomorrow, Lizzy, so let's turn in."

But for Lizzy, the night had just begun.

38

THE JOURNAL

WHILE WAITING FOR everyone else in the club to go to bed, Lizzy spread the printout of the journal on her dressing table and reread the parts relating to the dreadful Charles Mavroleon. Even though she knew the story well, she was still amazed at just how truly wicked he was.

The journal described how the handsome Mavroleon had been working for the East India Company at the same time as George was Resident of Junagadh and living secretly with Leela, his Indian wife.

Somehow Mavroleon found out, and visited their house in the hills above the city unexpectedly, openly flirting with her. To get him out of the way George took him on a lion-hunting expedition. Mavroleon callously shot three lion cubs, and George was so disgusted that he never hunted again. He managed to persuade the Nawab that he should make efforts to conserve the lions. "That was the only thing of value I ever accomplished," he wrote.

Then he had stolen the Moonstone and returned to England, where, having learnt of his beloved Leela's death, he recontacted his childhood sweetheart Penelope and proposed.

After their marriage they had returned to the remote North Yorkshire moors. Using her fortune, he remodelled the Tudor mansion that she had inherited into Shalimar as a memorial to his beloved Leela, hiding the Moonstone inside. He settled an annuity in trust for his son, who now went by the name of Christopher Jones …

And whatever happened to him? Lizzy thought.

Fifteen comfortable, childless years later a letter arrived for George from Mavroleon, threatening blackmail. He had discovered that George and Leela had actually been married in India and had a son—and he suspected that George would do anything to keep this from Penelope. They arranged to meet at the Oriental, and George took a large amount of cash with him to buy Mavroleon off.

The evening before George had left for London full of foreboding, he and Penelope had climbed up to Grimstone Scar, where they had met secretly as young lovers. There Penelope had asked George whether he truly loved her, and he had told her "Yes, more than I can say". She had stayed true and faithful to him all her life.

And my great-great-grandfather Titus was born nine months after, Lizzy noted with sigh. She looked up from the printed sheets. The sounds of loud after-dinner conversations and banging doors in the hallways still reverberated through the club.

She started reading the journal again.

When I met Mavroleon at the Oriental he confirmed my worst expectations. Wearing a shabby uniform, both bloated with drink and shrunk with the fever, he was a wreck of the handsome devil-may-care fellow I had last seen in India sixteen years before. We talked of old acquaintances in the bar, and then I told him we should adjourn to the Turkish baths where we could talk privately.

It was in the steam room there that he laid out his vile plot to me. He started on the lines I had expected—Penelope would be surprised to learn about Leela, he said. So she would, said I, but she was a grown woman and what was past was past. "Past!" he scoffed. "Why Leela is still alive, and your proper wife what's more. Do you think Penelope will understand that she has married a bigamist, and that he has a son by his other wife?" My heart beat furiously at his words. "But you wrote yourself to tell me that Leela had died," I cried, "and so did the Nawab ... "

I will never forget the thin, inhuman smile that played on Mavroleon's lips as he told me that he had invented Leela's death so that he might have her for himself, and had bribed the Nawab of Junagadh's scribe to forge the letter to confirm the tale. "It was Leela who told me you were married and had a child," he said. "She thought it would put me off ... but I had her anyway," he added maliciously.

"Then she is still alive?" I asked, aghast. "Saw her but five months ago," he replied. "Just before I left. And as good-looking a woman as she ever was. Now I wonder what your Penelope will make of her rival?" He looked at me with an expression of such cold, calculating depravity that I was left breathless. I excused myself for a moment, leaving Mavroleon to savour his moment of triumph.

What should I have done in such a situation? Hightailed to Yorkshire to beg forgiveness of Penelope on bended knee? Paid Mavroleon off in dirty cash and hoped to God that would be the last I saw of him? Perhaps either of these would have been a sensible solution, but I was insensible with the thought that my beloved Leela was still alive, and that this odious man had kept me from my greatest happiness for fifteen years.

What I did next was cruel—barbarous even. But I swear that if I had known then what I knew later, I would happily have devised a more ghastly fate for that malevolent swine. Gathering my wits despite the turmoil in my mind, I told the steward that my guest had departed and that, as was my custom, I would sleep that night in the frigidarium of the Turkish baths. He left, and I quickly returned to the steam room and jammed a mop through the door handles so that Mavroleon was shut within. Then I sought the temperature regulator in the boiler room and turned it to maximum.

It is no great pleasure to watch a man be steamed alive, but when that man is your sworn enemy and has kept you from your true love by his lies, the pill is sweetened. Mavroleon hammered against the glass doors, furiously at first but then more and more weakly; the mop held fast. Eventually I saw him dimly through the glass as he flopped to the floor, his tongue hanging out, trying to draw a cool breath from the gap underneath the door, mewling piteously. I sat in a canvas chair and watched, unmoved. If I had had a cheroot, I would have smoked it slowly, and snuffed it out gladly as the villain breathed his last.

It was done, and now I had to live with the consequences. I removed the mop and turned the regulator back down, but they were futile gestures: it would be known soon enough that I had murdered Mavroleon. God have mercy on my soul, but my only thought was for Leela. Would she forgive me once I had explained his vile imposture?

It was the work of a moment to put on my loose Indian clothes— like most members of the Oriental I preferred native attire at the club. I darkened my face, hands and feet with lampblack, and left through the servants' door …

Lizzy let the papers fall from her hands, wondering what might have been going through Uncle George's mind as he watched the man who had ruined his life suffer so terribly. Uncle George must have loved Leela very much. Despite the warmth she shivered at the thought of that boiled body splayed out on the marble floor …

Silence had descended on the club. She remembered what her real mission was.

She packed a rucksack with the printout of the journal and her notebook. Putting her torch in her trouser pocket, she opened the door of her room carefully and glanced down the corridor. There was nobody to be seen. She crept to the head of the staircase. Looking down two stories she could see the desk where the enormously fat night porter was gently snoring in his chair, the Chinese lacquered wall-clock ticking above him. She tiptoed down the stairs and stopped still as he shifted position slightly, but soon his rumbling resumed.

She was about to sneak across the hallway when there was a loud knocking at the front door. "Open up!" she heard from the outside. The porter stirred, grunted and hauled himself to his feet as the doors rattled and someone tried to get in.

"Comin', comin'," he muttered to himself, switching the lights on. As he waddled over to the door Lizzy dived for cover behind the four-armed statue of the elephant god. Two tall flushed-faced men in dinner jackets stood on the threshold supporting each other.

"Evening, Parsons," one slurred in greeting.

"Evenin', Sir James," the porter replied. "Evenin', Mr Guthrie."

"And a very good evening it was, too," Mr Guthrie finished with a loud hiccup. He and Sir James stumbled laughing through the door, as Parsons stepped to one side.

Having picked up their room keys, they stopped at the bottom of the stairs opposite the statue and looked at it blearily. Lizzy stood behind, immobile.

"Y'know what, Murray," Sir James slurred, "my grandfather had one jusht like 'im at Inverary. Ganesh, he's called."

"Really? Odd-looking blighter, isn't he? What does he do?"

"Do? He's a god, for Heaven's sake. He doesn't have to do anything!"

"He must do something, James. Cure warts or prevent rabies … "

"Oh, that sort of do!" Sir James exclaimed. "He's the Lord of Good Fortune. Brings good luck to any new undertaking, bless 'im … " He bowed low to Ganesh with his hands held together in front of him as if in prayer.

After the pair had weaved their way unsteadily up the stairs the porter switched off the main lights and was gazing blankly into space—the very space that Lizzy needed to cross to get to the library. She got down on hands and knees, and scarcely allowing herself to breathe she crawled like a cat along the front of the reception desk where he couldn't see her, the ticking clock matching her thumping heart. She made it to the library doors, reached up, and turned the handle.

And slipped silently in.

39

THE LIBRARY AT THE ORIENTAL

DARK WOOD BOOKCASES lined the walls, bulging with leather-bound volumes; their gold embossed titles glinted in the torchlight. Underneath the window was a large wooden case with lots of small drawers—it must be the card index of the books in the library, Lizzy thought. She walked over to look for the letter '*H*'.

"How many hours did I spend making notes in Colonel Hunt's *The Chronology of Creation?*" Uncle George had written—it was those notes that Lizzy needed to work out where the Moonstone was hidden.

George had heard rumours at the Oriental about a curse on the Moonstone, and had concealed it in an old priest's hole that he had found when he had remodelled Shalimar. He had made it so that the light of the full moon at the summer solstice would fall on it, "rebalancing the stone" as he thought, and eliminating the curse. But where was the priest's hole?

As she was searching for the '*H*' drawer the torchlight caught a curious object on top of the case, and the small brass plaque fixed to its base:

THIS TELLURIAN WAS RESPECTFULLY DONATED BY CHARLES SNODGRASS ESQ OF BENFIELD COURT, BERKS, TO THE ORIENTAL CLUB, JUNE 1845.

Tellurian! Uncle George had mentioned that as well ...

Below, in smaller letters, was written, '*Converted to Electricity by Order of the Committee, October 1905.*'

Lizzy flashed the torch onto the tellurian above, a beautiful scientific instrument made mainly of mahogany and brass. It consisted of a small globe showing the continents at the end of a long wooden arm that pivoted around a central light representing the sun. Neat strings and pulleys meant that as the globe circled on its arm around the sun, it also turned on its axis to simulate the earth's daily rotation. And spinning around the earth on the end of a brass rod was a little model of the moon the size of a small white marble.

Lizzy risked switching on the light, which sent a focused beam at the earth from the sun at the centre. She pushed a handle so that the earth did a complete circle around the sun, and although she didn't count, the earth span busily round on its tilted axis three hundred and sixty-five times as it completed its annual circuit, and the moon rotated slightly more than twelve times around the earth.

It was a marvel, Lizzy thought, like being in outer space and watching the cycles of the days and seasons and the phases of the moon all dancing to the music of time in front of your eyes. She kept the rotation going, smiling at the simple beauty of it all as simulated summer succeeded simulated spring and the moon waxed and waned before her. The movements of the earth and moon around the sun suddenly seemed so clear. Uncle George had learnt from it too, he had written. The full moon and the summer solstice, that was the clue …

As she looked at the tellurian Lizzy realised something— the full moon only occurred when the moon was on the opposite side of the earth to the sun—and so it was only visible at night, from the dark side of the earth. The full moon rose opposite the setting sun, and set opposite the sunrise. Sun and moon, equals and opposites—all at once what Uncle George had written in the journal about rebalancing the Moonstone started to make sense.

Switching off the light, Lizzy reluctantly tore herself away from looking at the tellurian, and resumed searching the index. She quickly found what she was looking for—'*The Chronology of Creation by Colonel Jocelyn Hunt, London 1829. XIV b. 392.*' The bookcases all had Roman numerals written on them in large letters—she quickly found XIV, and within moments was carefully carrying the heavy old book to the reading table in the centre of the room.

Lizzy opened the leather cover. Leafing through while holding the torch in the other hand wasn't easy. It was a large volume, with chapters on geology, botany and many other subjects; she consulted the index and found a chapter titled '*Cosmology: The Sun and Moon.*'

She heard voices and then the door swung open. Snapping off the torch, she ducked behind a sofa. Someone switched on a desk light. For a horrible moment Lizzy thought it might be Shankar …

"We will not be disturbed here," came the silky voice of a man.

A woman replied tersely in an Eastern-European accent. "To business, then. You know my requirements, Mr Streeter."

"Indeed, Countess Laszlo."

Lizzy peered cautiously round the sofa from the shadows. They were sitting at the table where *The Chronology of Creation* lay open, a man with a beard wearing a khaki waistcoat with pockets everywhere and a slim, elegant woman in a black dress topped by a hat from which hung a veil obscuring her face.

Mr Streeter placed a large sheet of blotting paper in front of him, and with a practised move, reached into his right breast pocket, and took out a black velvet bag. He poured the contents onto the blotting paper; scores of gemstones ran out like a river of brilliant green light.

"Emeralds," he said.

From his top left pocket he produced a bag which resulted in a stream of deep-red light.

"Rubies."

With a flourish he poured the contents of another bag onto the paper, blue this time.

"Sapphires." He glanced down complacently. "The big three in the coloured stones market."

"Spare me your lectures, Mr Streeter," the Countess said witheringly. She reached into her bag and produced an eyepiece which, lifting her veil, she placed to her eye. She picked up one of the largest rubies and examined it carefully.

"Jagdalak," she stated eventually.

"Yes, of course," Mr Streeter murmured, trying to hide the fact he was impressed that she had identified the mine in Afghanistan the ruby came from.

Countess Laszlo scrutinised a couple of emeralds without comment, then picked up the largest sapphire, looking at it long and hard. Mr Streeter seemed to Lizzy to be getting nervous: sweat appeared on his forehead, and his right leg was trembling. Finally the Countess put the eyepiece back in her bag and sat back in her chair.

"Mr Streeter, you vaste my time!"

"My dear Countess … " he started to protest, but she stood up.

"I told you no flaws. Do you take me for a fool?" she said imperiously. "Goodnight, Mr Streeter." She turned on her heels and swept out of the room. Mr Streeter carefully replaced all the stones in their bags muttering under his breath all the while.

When he had gone, Lizzy sighed with relief. Then a thought occurred to her. She got the printout of the journal from her rucksack and searched for a certain passage …

"This flaw in the Moonstone was the most strange thing," Uncle George had written, "The yellow diamond was afire with light from every angle—except one, where it was if the light was sucked into the stone, and it turned black. This was why the Moonstone was considered sacred in India— like the sun and the moon, it had the properties of both light and dark … "

It's strange, Lizzy thought, reflecting on what the Countess had said, *people don't like gems to have flaws, but the flaw is what makes the Moonstone sacred.*

Sun and moon. Light and dark. She looked at the tellurian, and was reminded of the work she still had to do …

As soon as she started to read the chapter on Cosmology, she knew she was on the right track. In the margins were pencilled notes in what she recognised as Uncle George's handwriting. She got her notebook and biro out of her pocket and started meticulously copying what he had written. A loud cough from the porter in the hallway made her jump, but she forced herself to concentrate.

The book itself had lots of very complicated astronomical detail about the orbits of the earth and moon around the sun, how they rotated, summer and winter solstices and mathematical formulae for calculating all these things. From his notes in the margins, it seemed that Uncle George had been trying to work out something very specific about the angle of the full moon on a summer solstice. He had noted that the full moon would follow exactly the same path through the sky as the sun did at the winter solstice. "The same but opposite … !" he had written. Lizzy thought how extraordinary it all was—she'd had no idea that the sun and moon behaved like mirrors of each other.

"Exact longitude and latitude of Shalimar?" one note read. If Uncle George had found this information, it wasn't written here. Lizzy sighed. There were clues in the notes, but still a lot more work to do. Looking at the mind-boggling formulae in the book, even the thought of trying to work these things out exhausted her. She yawned and looked at her watch—it was three o'clock in the morning. Satisfied that she'd noted down everything and checked it properly, she took out her rubber and carefully rubbed out all that Uncle George had written.

'That'll make it difficult for Shankar,' Lizzy said to herself with grim satisfaction. She was one step ahead of him for now, but she had to stay that way. She replaced the book on its shelf and opened the library door a fraction. The porter was busy doing suduko in a magazine, and looked wide awake. Better not try to get past him just yet, Lizzy thought, and found a comfortable leather armchair and promptly fell fast asleep.

It was already fully light and sparrows were twittering in the back courtyard outside the library when Lizzy was woken by a loud clatter from a trolley being wheeled down a corridor somewhere in the club. She rubbed her eyes and went to peek out the door. The porter wasn't anywhere to be seen so she skipped across the hall, ran up the staircase and went back to her room. She had just got undressed and climbed wearily into bed when there was a tap at her door.

"Mmmmm?" she mumbled.

"Lizzy, can I come in?" It was her father.

She sighed. "Yeah … "

He was looking horribly bright and cheerful. "I thought we'd make an early start, Lizzy," he said. "Plenty to see and do before we get the train back."

"Can't I sleep in?" Lizzy pleaded.

Her father looked disgruntled. "I've brought you to London as a special treat and all you want to do is look at the inside of your eyelids," he complained.

"Okay, okay!" Lizzy dragged herself unwillingly out of bed.

After she had washed and dressed she went to her father's room. They were about to leave together when the phone rang.

"Hello, Rose! What a pleasant surprise!" Her father smiled, and they started to chat away.

Rose! Lizzy had hardly thought about her, but suddenly she remembered what Josh had told her about the letter when they'd snatched half-an-hour together just after she came back from India. She had no more idea what the envelope addressed from Rose to Mabel Corker could mean than he did. It was strange enough that Uncle William should be keeping Mabel at the nursing home, but that Rose wrote letters to her as well? She shook her head. Sometimes she felt as if everyone involved in the Shalimar estate had secrets that she could only guess at. Well—she had secrets of her own too …

She could hardly keep her eyes open as they had breakfast in the dining room. Her father read the Sunday papers as Lizzy ate her kippers. She mulled over what she had discovered …

"Is there a priest's hole at Shalimar, Dad?" she blurted out suddenly. She'd meant to find a more roundabout way of asking her father, but her tiredness made her careless.

"What an odd question," her father remarked, peering over his reading glasses. "Why do you ask?"

"They mention a priest's hole in a book I'm reading," she improvised.

"Well, I've not heard of one at Shalimar, but the old house did belong to a big Catholic family once, so there might have been one before."

"Is a priest's hole big?"

"Depends on the size of the priest," her father answered with a grin. "Actually, sometimes they were large secret rooms, but mostly they were no bigger than a broom cupboard."

"Why did the priests have to hide?"

"Because Catholics were being persecuted by the Protestants and they weren't allowed to worship their way." Her father folded his newspaper, warming to his subject. "There's more strife been caused by religion than by anything else, Lizzy. I was just reading about this theme park they're building in Spain—OneWorld. They're trying to build bridges between all the world's religions, and … "

"It's all because of the sun and moon," Lizzy murmured, thinking of the journal.

"What is?" asked her father, puzzled. Lizzy sometimes came out with the strangest ideas ...

"*There are more things in heaven and earth ... than are dreamt of in your philosophy,*" she continued. They were amongst the last lines Uncle George had written.

"I didn't know you'd read *Hamlet,*" he said, looking pleased. Laythorpe College had really made a difference to her education.

"I haven't," replied Lizzy.

40

THE SUN AND THE MOON

L IZZY LOOKED OVER HER shoulder to make sure that no one had seen her, then walked gingerly onto the old cast-iron bridge across the river which pupils at Laythorpe College were forbidden to use.

She could see the Swale flowing underneath through the big holes in the rotten planking. The river was brown and swollen from the storms on the moors earlier in the week, and full of dead branches and vegetation. Peering over the intricate iron parapet, Lizzy threw a stone moodily into the water.

Some of that comes from Eden Beck, she thought, feeling homesick. After the success of their weekend together at the Oriental, her father had promised to let her come home for the term's final weekend out, but at the last moment he'd telephoned to say that it was Rose's birthday and they were going away together.

Virtually everyone at school had left with parents or friends, and Lizzy was fed up. She'd rung Josh, and he'd agreed to take the bus the next morning and meet her at Langbridge, the nearest town to the school. It meant that Lizzy had to sneak out and take the short cut across the river, but the thought of meeting him cheered her up.

With a new spring in her step she followed the track by the hawthorn hedge around the wheat fields.

"Now then, Lizzy," Josh grinned at her an hour later. He'd managed to make a cup of tea last until she showed up, but the owner of the Copper Kettle wouldn't let them sit there all day without ordering something.

"I'm starving!" Lizzy said. She hadn't felt like breakfast earlier, and the air was full of the smells of toasting bread and sizzling bacon. She looked at the menu, counted her money and worked out that she could afford egg on toast. "Do you want anything?" she asked Josh first, looking at him gratefully. He'd spent hours sitting on buses rattling down country lanes just because she'd asked him to.

"I'm fine. Me Mum made me a fry-up before I left." He'd had his hair cut shorter and had spiked it with gel, and his pale-blue eyes looked steadily at her. He seemed to have grown in confidence as well as height.

"How is she?"

"All right. Me Dad hurt 'is back but 'e's okay now."

"My Dad's gone away for the weekend with Rose."

"I know. You said," Josh replied evenly. "What do you reckon?"

"She's all right. I like her, but there's something a bit … I dunno."

"What about that letter she wrote to Mabel Corker?"

"I've no idea. But I'll tell you something … " Lizzy lowered her voice confidentially and looked around her to check that no one was listening in on their conversation.

"I know what the curse is."

Even the unflappable Josh was surprised. "W … w … what? 'Ow?" he stammered.

Keeping her voice down Lizzy told him what she'd read in the journal while Josh listened open-mouthed.

"You went to the Temple of the Moon," Josh said. "You told me—it was the one you had the dream about."

"Yeah, I know. It's really freaky."

"So you think the Moonstone is still at Shalimar?" he asked.

"I'm certain," Lizzy replied.

"'Ave you thought of telling your Dad about all this? Things are getting a bit hairy … "

"I can't," Lizzy said. "He'd tell Uncle William and Aunt Lavinia 'cause Shalimar's not our house to search. And if my Aunt got hold of the Moonstone she'd never let me take it back to the Temple … "

"Is that where you reckon it should go?"

"Absolutely! George regretted he'd never done that until his dying day."

"So somehow you've got to search Shalimar without anyone else knowing?"

"I know. But the Moonstone won't be easy to find." She got out her notebook and showed Josh what she'd copied from Uncle George's notes in the *Chronology of Creation*.

"It looks complicated," Josh said after he'd read the notes. "Angles, latitude and all that."

"Yeah. And the full moon only comes at the same time as the solstice once every thirty years."

"Your Uncle Peregrine would know about that, I reckon," Josh suggested. "They say 'e spends all 'is time looking at the sky through 'is telescope."

"Maybe he would," Lizzy said dubiously. She'd not seen her father's cousin since they'd met in the grove of cedars where her mother had died; she wasn't sure how he'd react if she called him out of the blue.

"And the light of the full moon on the solstice is supposed to 'it the stone in the old priest's 'ole? ... " Josh asked.

"Yup. So I need to know what the angle of the moon would be. It'll help us find the priest's hole."

"Yeah. You'd need to be a genius to work that out ... " Josh looked at Lizzy. "Or Ravi ... "

"I can't tell him about this." She explained what had happened with the scans. "I told him that the journal is too difficult for me to read just in case he tells Shankar."

"You think Shankar's after the Moonstone, too?" Josh asked.

"He must be."

"Well," Josh said, leaning back in his chair. "We'll just have to beat him to it."

"You'll help me?"

" 'Course."

There was something so reassuring about Josh, Lizzy thought. Nothing seemed to put him out—he even took the famous Shankar Pujari in his stride.

"I still think Ravi would be able to help you," Josh repeated after they'd mulled things over for a while. "You'd just 'ave to make sure 'e didn't know 'e was doing it."

They talked and looked at the notes, then talked some more. Eventually they came up with a plan.

Lizzy swallowed nervously as she phoned from school later that day. Although her father had given her Peregrine's number to ring in case of emergency, she didn't think this qualified as one.

"Hello?" a deep mellow voice responded.

"Ummm ... " Lizzy's voice trembled slightly.

"Is that Lizzy? I thought you'd call."

Lizzy started to wonder how he knew, but then remembered the incident by the weeping hornbeam. It seemed he always knew, somehow.

"Yeah, it is. I'm doing some astronomy at school and I wonder if you could help me?" she asked.

"Perhaps," Peregrine replied.

"It's about the sun and the moon ... "

"Hmmm. Everything is ... "

"I've been reading ... "

"There's no substitute for observation, Lizzy," Peregrine interrupted. "First we have to watch them with our own eyes to understand their movements and their deeper influences."

"Influences?"

"The sun does more to the earth than heat it, and there's more to the moon than the tides. You of all people should know that ... " It was the first time that Peregrine had hinted at anything to do with their strange meeting at Grimstone Scar, but it didn't sound as if he thought it had been anything out of the ordinary. "The ancients knew these things at first hand, from their own observations. Not from books."

"I know, but I need to find out something before the solstice," Lizzy said impatiently.

"The heavens can't be hurried," he replied. "I'll tell you one thing, however. It will be the full moon on the summer solstice this year. The moon will trace exactly the same path in the sky as the sun does at its winter solstice. Sun and the moon, the same, but opposite. That makes it a very special event. One that you should take care to observe."

After a brief goodbye, Peregrine put the phone down, and Lizzy scribbled what he had told her in her notebook. He had reminded her of something she had read in Uncle George's journal, and she got the printout from her desk drawer.

When ancient man first built civilisations by the side of great rivers, he had written towards the end, *he contemplated the interaction of those two most important celestial bodies, the sun and the moon. Small wonder he considered himself the centre of all creation; their cosmic dance is so beautifully staged for his delight, their size seen from earth so nearly the same, their movements equal and opposite. Perhaps all religions owe their genesis to the sun and moon, for only a god could preside over such perfection, and create man to meditate upon its glory.*

Lizzy didn't really understand the passage, but she sensed that there was more to her search for the Moonstone than just recovering a lost diamond. She felt part of the movement of the great unseen forces of the cosmos. Uncle George had written somewhere about rebalancing the stone … to Lizzy it felt as if the return of the stone would somehow rebalance—what? That she didn't know.

She sighed. It was all so complicated. But at least she had established one thing. The full moon would coincide with the solstice this year. It would be exactly as Uncle George had planned.

Later that night she couldn't sleep, and wandered through the empty, silent school towards the library.

She'd looked at just about every astronomy book in there without success, but she still hoped that she might find a solution to calculating the angle of the moon if she kept trying.

As she crossed the panelled hall, she noticed a light shining under the door of the headmaster's study. She stopped in her tracks, arrested by a sudden thought. She knew that Mr Hornchurch must be in there, but how did she know? She racked her brains. It was because he always insisted that pupils turned off the lights when they left a room. He hadn't, so he must be in there. Something about this niggled at Lizzy, and then it came to her …

The Moonstone! It was hidden in a priest's hole, but when the light of the full moon fell on it, '*the moonbeam at that moment would cause the diamond to light up with unequalled brilliance for a few minutes*,' Uncle George had written … Surely Lizzy would be able to find the whereabouts of the hidden priest's hole when the Moonstone lit up inside it! Shalimar was a huge house, but if she could just narrow down the possibilities …

41

CALCULATIONS

"HI, RAVI!" Lizzy greeted him with her sweetest smile. "Can I come in?"

"Yeah, of course," Ravi beamed at her. Ever since their disagreement over the scans Lizzy had been a little cool with him, and he was relieved that she seemed back to normal.

She sat down on the bed in his study. As usual Ravi was at his desk in front of his computer. "Listen, Ravi, I'm sorry, I went way over the top with that business with the scans."

"I shouldn't have done it, Lizzy," Ravi said. "Going behind your back like that."

"Anyway, I just wanted you to know that it really doesn't matter," Lizzy lied smoothly. "I can't read a word of the journal, even in the original."

"That's what Shankar told me, too." Ravi said.

"What!" Lizzy said.

"I saw him in London this weekend. He was staying with Mum and Dad—the music for *The Lifeline* is being recorded there."

"And he talked about the journal?"

"I asked him about it, actually," Ravi said. "Knowing how upset you'd been."

"And what did he say?"

"He told me the scans were impossible to read … "

He would, wouldn't he, Lizzy thought grimly.

"He asked if you'd managed to—" Ravi continued.

"Decipher it? Like I told you, I can't either—it's too difficult,"

"That's what I told him—I thought it's what you'd want me to say."

"Thanks. Not that it really matters now." Although she appreciated that Ravi was doing his best to make it up to her, Lizzy was thankful that she had kept her research into the journal from him. But this was bad news about Shankar being in London.

I bet he went to the Oriental, Lizzy said to herself. The librarian was bound to have told him that she'd been there. She was relieved that at least she'd managed to rub out Uncle George's notes in *The Chronology of Creation.*

" … And guess what?" Ravi added.

Lizzy shrugged. "What?"

"Your Aunt Lavinia rang up and asked them all to the Shalimar Solstice Ball."

Lizzy swallowed hard—she hadn't expected that. Managing a stiff smile for Ravi she said, "Great! It'll be nice to see them … "

He'll be watching me like a hawk, she thought grimly. She wished she could think of a way to persuade Aunt Lavinia to uninvite him, but she'd welcome Attila the Hun and Adolf Hitler to the solstice ball if it furthered her social ambitions.

"Funnily enough, Ravi," Lizzy said, "I wanted to ask you something about the Solstice Party. I'm thinking of making a surprise for everyone, and I need your help."

"What sort of surprise?"

"Duh! If I tell you it won't be a surprise, will it?"

Ravi grinned. It was nice to be back in Lizzy's good books.

"So what do you want me to do?"

"I want to know the angle of the sun when it's at its highest in the sky."

"At its zenith? Easy," said Ravi, firing up his computer. He rapped the keys and a website came up, which he peered at for a moment. "I'll need the latitude of Shalimar, though."

Lizzy was ready for that—she'd already consulted Google Earth on her laptop that afternoon. She got out her notebook. "It's latitude 54.3112 degrees."

Ravi tapped the number in. "The sun's zenith at Shalimar on the solstice will be at an angle of 59.1834 degrees." Lizzy wrote it down.

"What direction will that be?"

"South. Obviously." He sounded surprised that Lizzy didn't know.

"And what time?"

"Noon. You know, midday is called that 'cos it's the middle of the day."

"Thanks," she said, making as if she was about to leave. "Oh, by the way, I spoke to Josh on the phone and he asked me how the school cricket team did yesterday?"

"The results are up on the notice board … " Ravi replied, shutting down his computer.

"I don't know what on earth the scores mean. Would you look for me, Ravi?"

"Sure. But why don't you come with? … "

"I'll wait here. Then we can talk when you get back."

"Okay," Ravi agreed obligingly. Now that Lizzy was being friendly again, he wasn't going to argue.

233

When he had left, Lizzy sat down quickly at his computer and switched it back on. She found the astronomical site that Ravi had visited in the browser's history, and quickly surveyed it. There was a box marked "Winter Solstice" and she clicked it, then feverishly entered the latitude of Shalimar and pressed 'Enter'. The result came back straight away—"12.6834 degrees at the zenith." She was scribbling it down when she heard Ravi's footsteps coming back down the corridor. Like lightning she went to the 'Clear History' menu on the browser, pressed it and shut the computer down. She just had time to resume her seat when he walked in.

"Laythorpe had scored one hundred and ninety-seven runs chasing two hundred and thirty-four with three wickets in hand when stumps were drawn," Ravi reported.

"Whatever that means."

"It means it was a draw."

"Sounds thrilling … I'll tell Josh. Thanks a lot, Ravi." Lizzy stood up to leave.

"Hey … !" Ravi shouted as she closed the door behind her. "I thought you wanted to talk!"

"We're getting there, Josh," Lizzy told him when she rang him that evening, "The priest's hole must be somewhere on the south side of the house. Which is that?"

Josh thought for a moment. "It's the side facing the stables," he replied.

Lizzy pictured that side of Shalimar in her mind's eye. It overlooked the Mughal Garden and was where all the principal rooms faced. She imagined standing on the terrace outside the French windows and then … something didn't fit. Frowning, she looked at the bit of paper on which she'd drawn an angle of 12.5 degrees. It was a very shallow angle, which surely meant that even at its maximum height the moon would be hidden by the stables built on the small rise nearby?

"Have you got a protractor?" she asked Josh. She could hear him fiddling around at the other end of the line.

"Got one!"

"Well, take a bit of paper and draw an angle of 12.5 degrees. It's near enough the angle the moon will be at— the same as the sun at the winter solstice."

There was a silence. Lizzy could almost hear Josh concentrating.

"Right! That's done," he told her shortly.

Lizzy considered for a moment. "Okay can you take it with you onto the roof of the stables right now?"

"I don't see why not—it's still light enough," came the reply.

"Imagine the moon at 12.5 degrees above the horizon, and tell me where you'd have to be in Shalimar to see it over the roof of the stables."

"I think I understand … "

"Good. Then call me right back."

The next ten minutes seemed to last for ever. But then her mobile rang.

"You couldn't see the moon from anywhere on the ground floor!" he confirmed.

Lizzy struggled to contain her excitement. "That means the priest's hole has to be on the first floor. Dad told me the old Tudor house didn't have any attics." Lizzy thought feverishly. "Josh?"

"Yeah?"

"I've got an idea, but we have to wait until the night of the Shalimar Ball."

"Why?"

"I can't explain now. But make sure you're free to be with me at midnight."

"Makes you sound like Cinderella," Josh said.

"Don't be daft!" Lizzy grinned as she put the phone down. For the first time she was really convinced that they could pull it off.

But then she remembered Shankar, and her blood ran cold.

42

THE SHALIMAR SOLSTICE BALL

Lizzy's father picked her up from school at the end of term, but the Sams insisted that Ravi went with them in Uncle William's Bentley and he couldn't really say no.

The next day was gloriously sunny, and in the morning Lizzy walked across the park to Stable Cottage. She explained her plan for the Ball that evening to Josh and they went through it over and over again to make sure that they hadn't forgotten anything. Aunt Lavinia hadn't invited him or his parents to the party, of course, so they arranged to meet at the back of the house at a-quarter-to midnight.

As she was walking home Lizzy couldn't resist checking out what was happening at Shalimar. It was a hive of activity—Aunt Lavinia was outside the front door ordering the caterers, gardeners and florists around like a conductor with an orchestra, and neighbours kept dropping in, pretending to see if they could help.

"Lavinia, my dear," gushed Hortensia Ochterlony, "How lovely everything looks! I'm sure your guest will be enchanted … Is he here yet?" She had come specially hoping to get a sneak preview of the famous author.

"Not yet. William's picking him up from Knowlesby station just before the party," Lavinia replied, pruning some

237

roses with her secateurs. "Lizzy, your father tells me he's bringing ... Who is that teacher again?"

"Rose," Lizzy said.

"That's it, Rose. What a sweet name." She pursed her lips as she clipped a limp pink bloom off a bush.

"Cleo will be disappointed if I don't get his autograph," Hortensia persisted. Her daughter had threatened to go on a hunger strike if she failed ...

"Oh, we don't want to bother him with autographs," Lavinia told her haughtily. "He's here as our private guest, not for show." She didn't add that she had made certain that everyone knew that the celebrated Shankar Pujari would be coming to her party.

Lizzy suppressed the urge to laugh, and instead walked round to the south side of the house. She looked at the stables on the hillside opposite—if her calculations were correct, by midnight the full moon would have risen above the roof and would shine onto Shalimar. She scoured the first floor of the house for any sign of the shaft Uncle George had drilled to let the moonbeam into the priest's hole. There was nothing to be seen.

Not for the first time she wondered whether she had dreamt the whole thing.

Lizzy's father put the phone down. He was ready to go to the ball, dressed in the smart black dinner jacket which Alice had always thought made him look so handsome.

"That was Rose," he told Lizzy. "She's been delayed—unavoidable, she said. And when—if—she comes, she's bringing someone she says I absolutely have to meet."

"Lavinia won't like that," Lizzy said. Her aunt was very fussy about who came to the party.

"Well, that can't be helped." He sighed. "Rose is being very mysterious, I must say."

The sun disappeared behind Eden Great Moor as they walked through the park up to Shalimar. It was a warm, clear evening, and the swallows swooped through the air, catching insects. By tradition the midsummer party didn't start until sunset—nearly ten o'clock at that time of year—but her father wanted to be there a bit before in case any of the few guests he had been allowed to invite arrived early.

While he went through the front door to check who was on the guest list Lizzy walked round the side of the house to the garden entrance of the Durbar Hall. It was the first time she'd been back there since her Christmas outburst. Uncle William was standing just inside with his back to her.

"Good evening, Uncle William! How are you?" she said politely. He winced as soon as he heard her voice. When she was out of harm's way at school he could forget all about Lizzy, but here ...

"Excuse me, I am rather busy at the moment," he said, walking away purposefully.

"I'm very well, thank you!" she said sarcastically, putting out her tongue at his retreating back.

"Talking to yourself as usual?" Ravi said, appearing from behind the door. He looked very dashing in his black dinner jacket, which showed off his glossy black hair and dazzling white teeth. He whistled appreciatively. "Wow! You look great!"

"Thanks. And you've brushed up pretty nicely yourself."

Ravi grinned. He was learning to appreciate Lizzy's Yorkshireisms.

"Your mum had this made for me in Mumbai," Lizzy said, looking down at her dark-blue silk trouser suit. The jacket was in the high-collared Indian style, and her hair was tied back, showing her slender neck and pale skin. The tan she'd got in India had long since faded as she'd hardly spent any time outdoors during the summer.

They stood together near the double doors leading onto the north lawn watching the first guests arrive at the Durbar Hall. Her father strolled in at the other end, chatting to a sandy-haired, freckly man who Lizzy recognised as Alistair MacMillan. He'd been his father's best man at her parent's wedding. He stopped dead when he saw Lizzy, then walked over and embraced her warmly. "Good heavens, Lizzy," he said, holding on to her shoulders and examining her closely, "You're the spitting image of your … " He clammed up suddenly, concerned how Henry might react. He needn't have worried …

"She's just like Alice, isn't she?" Lizzy's father said. Alistair relaxed, and Lizzy introduced him to Ravi. As they talked about their trip to India, where Alistair had once worked as an aid doctor, the Durbar Hall started to fill up with new arrivals.

The Shalimar Midsummer Ball was the highlight of the North Yorkshire social calendar, more eagerly awaited than York Races, the White Rose Dinner and the Great Yorkshire Show put together. Even if they didn't know them personally, William and Lavinia asked all the high society of the county who almost invariably accepted, gladly donning their dinner jackets and ball gowns for the event. Famous sportsmen and women, wealthy businesspeople, distinguished judges and celebrity artists, writers and musicians all rubbed shoulders with the big landowners of the neighbourhood. Four hundred people had been invited, and not one failed to come.

But Shankar Pujari was the star. A hush fell on the Durbar Hall as Lavinia led him in, dressed in a black-silk dinner suit which hung elegantly off his tall, lean frame. She introduced him to the Lord-Lieutenant, Sir Fenwick Skrimshaw, the Chairman of Baines Breweries. He was the Queen's official representative for the county, and Lavinia had been trying for years to get him and his wife, Lady Hilda, to come to the Ball. Shankar was his usual charming, suave self, and soon they were talking away like old friends.

William looked at his wife proudly. Thanks to her the Durbar Hall looked spectacular, and the organisation was faultless, as always. And now that the Skrimshaws had accepted an invitation she had finally climbed to the very top rung of the social ladder, from which giddy heights she could look down upon all those who might once have looked down on her.

Leaving Shankar to chat to the Lord-Lieutenant and his wife, Lavinia stood with William by the doors greeting the guests as they flooded into the Durbar Hall. She lapped up their compliments when they gasped at the sight of the great candelabra with its scores of white candles sending dazzling light shooting in all directions from the stainless steel flames.

Rajesh Jog—the artist who sculpted it—had been invited to the party along with his glamorous wife, and Lavinia stationed him near at hand so that he could answer questions about it. She was thrilled to see James Hamilton, the gossip columnist for *Yorkshire Life*, talking to him. That would surely lead to a feature in the magazine—their photographer was busy snapping the inside of the hall with its decorations and huge bunches of white lilies standing in tall brass Indian vases.

Everything was going to plan, Lavinia thought complacently, when she was confronted with the sight of a large man with a pink face who had obviously struggled to fit into his dinner jacket.

"Evening, Mrs Abercrombie," he said shaking hands, his grip rather too firm for comfort. "You won't remember me. Chief Superintendent Briggs, as I was then ... "

"Ah yes, of course," Lavinia murmured politely. She didn't have the faintest idea who he was.

"I was called here after Alice Abercrombie's death a few years back, you may recall."

Lavinia looked at him again. How unpleasant of him to remind her of such things, she thought. She smiled thinly.

"We're delighted to see you under more congenial circumstances, Chief Superintendent."

"Chief Constable now," Briggs corrected her proudly as he presented his homely, blushing wife. Then he moved on to let the new arrivals through.

"Lizzy!" Shankar beamed when he spotted her, and the crowd around him respectfully gave way as he made his way over. "How delightful it is to see you," he said, taking her hands.

"Hello!" Lizzy smiled. "Ravi told me you were coming to the party. India seems ages ago, doesn't it?"

"Indeed it does! By the way, I'd still love a copy of that journal some time."

"Oh, I'm so sorry!" Lizzy said. "I clean forgot. But I haven't managed to read a word anyway. Uncle George writes like a drunken spider."

Shankar laughed expansively, but did Lizzy catch a tinge of suspicion in his cold eyes?

She felt a tap on her shoulder, and turned to find the Sams who were dressed in matching black-velvet dinner suits. Their resemblance was spookier than ever—Samuel's hair was cut short and Samantha had tied hers back severely so that it looked exactly like his.

They didn't bother to say hello.

"Introduce us!" Samantha hissed, nodding in the direction of Shankar.

"Yes, cuz, he's our guest, not yours," Samuel whispered, all the while smiling at Shankar.

Lizzy sighed wearily. "Shankar, these are my cousins Samantha and Samuel."

"Ah! I have heard all about you from your mother," Shankar said as he shook hands—the Sams could hardly believe that they'd finally met him. "How lucky you are to live in such a wonderful house!"

"Yah," Samuel drawled, "I suppose so. I've got used to it, really. Being brought up here and all." He looked pointedly at Lizzy.

"I don't think I'd ever get … " Shankar started.

"Samuel's going to inherit it when Dad dies," Samantha said. "But I'm going to live here as long as I want."

"Yah, of course, until you get married," Samuel agreed.

Samantha looked at him sharply. "But you said I could stay … "

"Can't have you cluttering the place up with your scream-ing brats, Sammy," Samuel added, smirking at Samantha.

He looked at Shankar expectantly for his approval.

"Yes, well, how fascinating … " Shankar forced a smile. "Excuse me a moment, I have just seen someone I have to talk to." He turned on his heels and walked off, the Sams watching his retreat indignantly.

"Bloody rude!" Samantha puffed.

"Yah!"

"I bet you really bored him, Lizzy,"

"Yah, she did, didn't she!"

"Did I see you talking to Shankar, darlings?" Lavinia asked as she appeared at their sides. "Isn't he simply charming?"

"He was until she showed up," Samantha curled her pretty lip. "She was bloody rude."

Lavinia turned on Lizzy in a cold fury. "I hope you're not going to pull another of your unforgivable stunts like last Christmas, young lady! If you dare—" Lavinia switched to a warm smile in an instant when she saw who was approaching. "Ah, KK have you met the Sa—"

"Here you are, Lizzy, my little star!" he said, embracing her. "Where have you been hiding?"

"Hello, KK!" Lizzy grinned with pleasure.

"I spent most of last week watching you!"

"What do you mean?" Lizzy asked, puzzled.

"I've been cutting the trailer for the film … it ends with you galloping across the screen." He put on a rich, deep film-trailer voice, miming with his hand the movement of a galloping horse on an imaginary screen. "Drmm drmm ENSIGN FILMS PRESENTS drmm drmm A FILM BY KK CHANDRA drmm drmm FROM THE BEST-SELLING BOOK BY SHANKAR PUJARI drmm drmm THE LIFELINE drmm drmm drmm drmm THE EXPERIENCE OF A LIFETIME!" He smiled at Lizzy.

"And believe you me, it has been! I am absolutely shattered." He turned to Lavinia and apologised. "Excuse me, Lavinia, I just had to tell her! These two youngsters must be Samuel and Samantha!" He shook their hands. "I'm delighted to meet you!"

Lavinia looked perplexed. "I don't understand. Are you saying Lizzy is actually in your film?"

"Oh, yes! Hasn't she told you?"

"I haven't seen her since she got back from India—but twins," she added, "you never told me this."

"What's to tell? It's only the trailer … " Samantha pouted.

"Only the trailer!" KK threw his head back and laughed uproariously. "She's in the film as well, of course, but that only goes out on the screen where it's shown. Whereas the trailer will go out on just about every screen in every multiplex and cinema on earth! Not forgetting TV and DVD! There won't be anyone from Madagascar to Mongolia who won't see Lizzy!"

The Sams were green with envy, and Lavinia went very silent.

"Anyway, you must excuse me if I drag her away from you—Kitten has been dying to see her … " KK took Lizzy by the arm and led her through the nearby guests who had been listening in attentively. Lizzy could hear a rising wave of excited conversation behind her …

The Sams were livid.

"It's all your fault," groaned Samuel. "It was you who lent her Stetson! She'd never have got any good at riding otherwise!"

"My fault! It was your stupid idea! You should have got her off!"

"Darlings! … " Lavinia anxiously tried to calm them down. People were staring.

"If you'd whipped him harder!"

"If she'd fallen like you said, at least she'd have broken her stupid neck."

"Darlings! … " People were starting to move away in distaste as the Sams glared at each other, breathing heavily.

"Everything all right, my sweet?" William asked as he shuffled up to Lavinia's side.

No, she thought, blinking back a tear of frustration. *Everything isn't.*

"Henry!" Hortensia Ochterlony stopped and kissed him on both cheeks. "What's this I hear about your Lizzy in *The Lifeline*?"

"Oh, that," Henry replied vaguely. "I don't know really— she hasn't told me much about it."

"Well, Cleo and Archie tell me it's all over Laythorpe and everyone's gone mad about riding as a result!"

"Have they?"

"And I just overheard someone saying that she's going to be seen absolutely everywhere … "

"Really?" said Henry, baffled.

Hortensia patted his cheek. "You really must keep a better eye on your lovely daughter, Henry. And do you think by any chance she could get me Shankar's autograph? … "

Kitten was talking to the Lord-Lieutenant and his wife when Lizzy and KK joined them.

246

"Lizzy! Oh God, you look beautiful!" Kitten was wearing a glittering gold sari that made her shimmer like a mirage. "This is the young lady I was telling you about, Sir Fenwick … "

The Lord-Lieutenant smiled at her. "So you're the lass who's a lion tamer … "

"It wasn't really like that—" Lizzy started to explain, but Kitten interrupted.

"She won't hear of it, but as far as I'm concerned she saved my son's life!"

"A modest lion-tamer?" Sir Fenwick said. "That's a rum combination if ever there was one!"

Lizzy excused herself after a while to go and get a drink from the bar in the marquee on the lawn. Lavinia had naturally hired the most glamorous one imaginable, festooned with fabulous Indian fabrics and lit by brass oil lamps like something out of Ali Baba's cave. Musicians sat cross-legged on a carpet on the stage in the middle, playing tabla drums and curious long-necked stringed instruments while a barefoot bejewelled woman danced slowly with extraordinarily graceful and eloquent gestures.

Lizzy watched, entranced.

"Hello!" Peregrine appeared at her shoulder with a glass of champagne in hand. He was wearing a loose-fitting dark-blue-velvet dinner jacket with a fantastically coloured floppy bow tie.

"Hello," Lizzy replied, pleased to see him. His grey eyes shone from his lean handsome face as he listened to the music. He looked so much more relaxed than all the other men in their stiff penguin suits. "Are you having a good time?"

"It's a very special occasion. A good time doesn't come into it."

"I meant the party … "

"I know you did. But I meant something else."

He moved away, then suddenly turned back. "Remember, Lizzy—observe!" he said, melting into the crowd.

Maud Batty walked past dressed in a pinny and little maid's cap, carrying a silver tray with rattling glasses of champagne on it. She bit her lower lip, staring at the glasses, willing them not to tip over.

"Hello, Maud," Lizzy said gently.

She glanced up and smiled. "Oh, 'ello, it's you Lizzy. Sorry—can't stop."

As Maud tottered slowly on, Lizzy looked at her watch. The time was fast approaching.

Alistair MacMillan caught up with Henry near the bar.

"What's all this about Lizzy the Lion Tamer, Henry?" he asked, taking a pakora from a tray. "Nobody seems to be talking about anything else."

Henry looked blank. "I honestly haven't got a clue. It seems I'm always the last to find out what Lizzy's up to."

"Well, that gorgeous Indian lady … "

"Kitten Chandra … "

"That's the one. She's been telling everyone that Lizzy saved her son from a lion in India."

"That's the first I've heard of it … " Henry downed his drink. He was beginning to think that there were things about his daughter that he hardly knew anymore.

Lizzy made her way back into the Durbar Hall where the party was in full swing. She stood by the fireplace keeping a close watch on Shankar, who in turn seemed to shoot occasional glances in her direction—or was she imagining it?

"Hi, Lizzy!" Ravi walked over and stood next to her. "Having fun?"

"Fine … " Lizzy answered vaguely, watching Shankar out of the corner of her eye as he moved behind one of the marble pillars of the hall.

"What do you mean, fine, Lizzy?" he asked with amusement. "Fine weather, fine cut like in cricket or fine feelings, like our friend the Raja said … "

It was all right. Shankar was only helping himself to a drink …

"Remember you promised to dance with me later?" Ravi said.

"Fine … " Lizzy repeated automatically. She checked her watch anxiously.

"When you've returned to planet earth, of course … " Ravi said as he moved away.

The disco started in the marquee at half-past eleven— Samantha immediately made a beeline for Ravi and dragged him protesting onto the dance floor.

"HELP!" he mouthed silently at Lizzy when he spotted her walking past.

A friend in need … Lizzy glanced her watch and sighed. She tapped Samantha on the shoulder, who turned, eyes blazing.

"Go away, cuz! Can't you see I'm busy?"

"Shankar's looking for you," Lizzy told her. "He's in the Mughal Garden."

Samantha was torn between celebrity and Ravi, and celebrity won. She ran out of the marquee without a backwards glance.

Ravi looked duly grateful, and clearly expected Lizzy to keep dancing, but she simply said "Sorry! See you later!" and left him stranded alone in the middle of the dance floor.

As she walked through the Durbar Hall people kept trying to ask her about lions and films. Her newfound fame was endangering her plan, and she had to be quite rude to some guests to be able to get away.

Then she was alarmed to see Shankar standing alone for a change, and she grabbed Hortensia Ochterlony by the arm as she was walking by.

"You must meet Shankar Pujari," she said, and introduced them.

She should keep him busy! she thought as she slipped quietly out of the Durbar Hall.

It was a-quarter-to-twelve.

She made her way down the long dark passage to the back of the house, and slid back the big old bolt on the heavy oak door.

Josh was waiting outside, and followed her without a word. They were about to pass the kitchen when the door opened and Tindy Postlethwaite stepped into the passage, blocking their way.

"What's he doing here?" she demanded, indicating Josh with a jerk of her head.

"It's none of your business," Lizzy retorted defiantly. "Get out of our way, please."

The sour-faced housekeeper hesitated, weighing up the options for a moment, then reluctantly stepped aside.

"Thank you very much!" Lizzy said as she pushed past with Josh.

"Mrs Abercrombie will hear of this!" Mrs Postlethwaite shouted after their retreating backs. "You can be sure she'll have words to say!"

They went through the hall and crept up the main staircase, leaving the sounds of music and laughter from the Durbar Hall echoing below. A couple of table lamps lit the south-facing drawing room, and Lizzy went through to turn them off. Looking out over the Mughal Garden, she was surprised that she couldn't see the moon. She checked her watch again. Six minutes to midnight and a clear night. Why wasn't it visible yet?

She drew the long curtains over the huge bay window and went out onto the landing. Josh had done the same in the main bedroom, and Lizzy went through to the guest bedroom to draw them in there. Her heart started to beat faster when she saw the domed four-poster: it was here she had first heard about the curse, and then dreamt about the Temple of the Moon …

Three minutes to midnight.

She went back to where Josh was waiting. Only the dim light from below showed where they were.

The minute hand of her watch edged closer to midnight.

"Now!" Lizzy whispered.

They circulated quickly and silently around the ink-black rooms looking out for a light shining through a chink in the panelling to betray the hiding place of the Moonstone.

Barely able to draw breath, Lizzy padded swiftly backwards and forwards between the drawing room and the guest bedroom to one side, her every nerve alert to the possibility of an unexplained ray of light. She could sometimes make out Josh's shadowy form as he concentrated on the main bedroom and the landing.

Midnight, and still no sign.

She nearly bumped into Josh in the dark. "Have you found anything?"

"Nothing!" he whispered.

"Me neither! We're running out of time!" Lizzy said.

They resumed their search, banging into furniture and tripping over carpets in their haste.

Two minutes past midnight. Uncle George had written that the light would only last a few minutes …

It was ten-past midnight when Lizzy was finally convinced that they had failed.

Suddenly there was a series of loud explosions, and brilliant light flashed through a crack in the curtains in the drawing room.

Lizzy tore them open …

And she stood open-mouthed at the fantastic firework display bursting over the Mughal Gardens.

They stepped out onto the balcony. Huge rockets soared into the air and exploded in incandescent showers, Catherine wheels whirred, their reflections in the water of the formal ponds spinning madly, and the clear night air was filled with flashes and bangs. They watched as the spectacle reached its climax and the guests below cheered and clapped.

And then Lizzy saw the full moon shining through the trees to the left of the stables. It was too low, wasn't it? And too far to the left …

She tried to work out what had gone wrong. She must have made a mistake about the angle, or maybe the latitude. But she'd checked and double-checked, hadn't she?

"I'm sorry, Lizzy," Josh said.

"It's not your fault," Lizzy replied miserably. She took a deep breath. "C'mon, let's go and dance."

"But I can't, Lizzy," Josh protested as she led him by the hand down the staircase. "Look what I'm wearin'!"

"You look great!" Lizzy reassured him. He wore surfer shorts and a baggy T-shirt, his blond hair was spikily gelled, and he looked lankier than ever.

"But everyone else is dressed up!"

"And they all look stupid, Josh. Honest!"

"Your aunt will have me guts for garters!"

"She won't. Trust me!"

In fact no one batted an eyelash when Lizzy stepped onto the dance floor with Josh. The party was a roaring success and everyone was out to enjoy themselves as much as possible. Lizzy threw herself into dancing with a vengeance. She wanted to blow everything out of her mind—the journal, the Moonstone, Uncle George, the curse. You failed, forget it, have fun! Josh was a great dancer, too, and they danced on and on until …

"What the hell are you doing here?" Samuel shouted in Josh's ear. Lizzy pushed him away.

"He's with me," she said.

"I can see that!" Samuel replied. "He's not allowed … "

"I've allowed him!"

"I'm going to tell my mother," Samantha said, joining the fray.

"See if I care!"

"Lizzy … " Josh pleaded, "I really don't want to cause—"

"It's them who are the trouble!" She glared at the Sams.

"That's as may be," Josh said, "but I'm not sticking around to find out." With a rueful shrug, he stalked off the dance floor, the crowd closing behind him.

"I'll tell Mum anyway—she'll sack them!" Samantha smirked.

"You do that, and I'll make sure Ravi never speaks to you again! Ever!" Lizzy said.

Samantha turned on her heels, tight-lipped.

"You haven't seen Rose, have you Lizzy?" her father asked her as she bumped into him in the hallway. "She still hasn't shown up … "

"No, I haven't … Have you seen Josh?" She'd looked for him everywhere.

"No … Is he here?"

"He was." Lizzy sat down on one of the carved teak benches with a sigh. Her father sat next to her.

"It's been quite an evening," he reflected.

"Yeah, I suppose so." She'd abandoned any hope of finding the Moonstone, but the disappointment still sat like a lead weight in her stomach.

"I've been hearing a lot of stories about you!" her father said. Lizzy looked at him. He hadn't heard about their Moonstone search, had he? Not that it made any difference now. "Seems you have been up to all sorts of things I didn't know about," he continued.

"Yeah, well," Lizzy hung her head.

"You don't have to be modest with me, Lizzy." Her father put his arm around her shoulders. "I'm really proud of you—and especially of what you did to save Ravi … "

"Eh?" So he wasn't talking about the Moonstone after all …

" … There's a cool head on those young shoulders of yours, Lizzy." He beamed at her. It was ages since she'd seen such warmth in his eyes. "I wonder what 'Lion' Abercrombie would have made of his great-great-great-granddaughter the lion-tamer … " her father said, nodding in the direction of Uncle George's portrait on the landing.

"I'm not a lion-tamer—" Lizzy started to protest, but her father interrupted.

"I know, I know, Kitten's rather prone to exaggeration, but I got the whole story from the horse's mouth, so to speak. Ravi filled me in. He's a nice boy … " He watched Lizzy, weighing her reaction.

She looked away. They sat in companionable silence for a moment, both gazing at the portrait. The sad faraway look in Uncle George's eyes seemed to draw Lizzy in. Having read the journal, for the first time she felt that she really understood him.

"Pity George turned out to be such a rotter … " her father remarked.

"He didn't mean to abandon Leela. He was tricked," Lizzy said.

"What do you mean, Lizzy?" her father asked, intrigued.

" … And tricked again into abandoning Penelope. He paid for it for the rest of his life." She shook her head. She felt as if the fate of Uncle George was inextricably entwined with her own …

"How do you—" her father started saying, but then a voice boomed out:

255

"Lizzy! Here you are! I was looking for you everywhere!" KK appeared in the hallway with Kitten and Ravi not far behind. "I got your aunt to delay the fireworks because you were nowhere to be found. I didn't want my star to miss them!"

"It's okay, thanks, I saw them. They were great!"

"They were, weren't they?" Kitten sat down on the bench next to her. "I haven't had such a good time since … Oh God, I don't know when!"

"Would you like to dance, Lizzy?" Ravi asked. "You promised you would."

"Okay," Lizzy responded without much real enthusiasm. She was still concerned about what had happened to Josh. She hated the idea of him being forced to retreat by her vile cousins.

Lavinia's thin high laugh could be heard above the buzz of the conversation in the Durbar Hall. It always got louder the angrier she was, and by now she was really seething. Not only had Shankar and KK ignored the Sams and they'd argued in front of everyone, but all the guests were talking about Lizzy this and Lizzy that—it was driving her mad. And to cap it all KK had insisted that she held up the start of the fireworks—they always started at midnight—until Lizzy could be found, and of course the wretched girl had gone missing. Tindy Postlethwaite said she'd caught her sneaking down a back corridor with Josh Giddons—the groom's son, for Heaven's sake! Then they'd been seen dancing together, and he was dressed like a beach bum!

What a disaster! …

And now Lady Hilda Skrimshaw was praising Lizzy to the skies for saving Ravi's life, of all ridiculous things.

"It's simply preposterous!" Lavinia laughed maniacally.

"The stories that girl makes up about herself!"

Lady Hilda's brow furrowed.

"I blame William," Lavinia continued. "He's generous to a fault, of course, and he insisted that Lizzy go to Laythorpe College and he even pays for her! That's the kind of man he is! His brother Henry can't afford it—he's some sort of third-rate scientist. The whole boarding school thing has simply gone to Lizzy's head, I'm afraid. She's just not used to mixing in decent circles—"

"It was Kitten who told us, not Lizzy," Lady Hilda interrupted firmly.

"Oh, Kitten! Frankly, I haven't much time for her!" Lavinia had a terrible feeling that she was going too far but she couldn't stop herself. "So flighty and unreliable!"

"She's a charming woman ... and Shankar confirmed the story—"

"Well he would, wouldn't he? He's as thick as thieves with the Chandras ... "

"And these thieves are all staying at Shalimar?" Lady Hilda enquired with an acid smile. "How kind of you to accommodate them!" She turned to her husband. "Fenwick, I've got a terrible earache all of a sudden. We must leave."

"As you like, luv!" Sir Fenwick sighed with relief. William Abercrombie had been angling for an invitation to his shoot for the last half-hour.

"It's all right," Lady Hilda said as Lavinia started to follow them, "we'll show ourselves out, thank you ... Mind those thieves don't pinch the silver, now!"

"What was that about, my precious?" William asked, baffled. He'd been getting on really well with Sir Fenwick, so he thought.

257

"That woman is so rude!" Lavinia sniffled. "I never want her to set foot in this house again! It's all Lizzy's fault! You've got to take her out of Laythorpe, William. I insist!"

William's face suddenly darkened with fury. He grabbed Lavinia by the wrists.

"You're hurting … !" she cried.

"If I say Lizzy stays at Laythorpe, she stays," he said savagely. "And after she can go to university wherever she wants with my blessing—and my money. Got that?"

Lavinia looked at her husband in fright. All the stress of the evening, and now William was acting like a brute …

Her face turned red, crinkling like burning cellophane. She burst into tears.

Lizzy danced with Ravi while Samantha watched from a corner, fuming.

He's a really hopeless dancer, Lizzy thought as he flailed his legs and arms about, but she kept going. She'd promised, after all …

Then she spotted a spiky hairdo pushing through the crowd, and the next thing she knew Josh was standing in front of her panting.

"Lizzy! You've got to come quick!" he yelled above the music.

"Hey! This is my dance!" Ravi protested as Josh took Lizzy by the hand and dragged her off the dance floor.

"What is it?" Lizzy shouted.

"The moon! It's nearly where you told me it should be!"

"What?"

They pushed their way through the guests into the Durbar Hall, ignoring Watch-where-you're-goings and sarcastic Excuse-mes.

They ran into the hallway. Lizzy suddenly skidded to a halt on the white-marble floor.

"Uncle Peregrine!" she cried. He was just about to go up the stairs. He paused, and looked at Lizzy. "Did ... did you see the full moon?" she stammered.

"Not yet," he said, unruffled as ever. "That's why I'm going up on the roof."

"But ... but the zenith was at midnight, wasn't it?" Lizzy asked.

He laughed. "Much use all your books have been, Lizzy. Didn't you put your clocks forward at the end of March?"

Lizzy was aghast. She'd completely forgotten that they were on Summer Time. "So the zenith is at one o'clock?" She glanced down at her watch. It was three minutes past already ... Her heart sank.

"Not quite," Peregrine explained. "There are Shalimar's longitude and the equation of time to consider as well."

Lizzy grabbed his sleeve. "So when is it? Exactly?" she pleaded.

Her urgency registered, and Peregrine suddenly became serious. "Seven minutes past one, give or take a few seconds. But why, Lizzy?"

His question went unanswered. Lizzy bolted up the stairs with Josh hot on her heels.

Shankar looked up from the doorway of the Durbar Hall, an odd smile on his thin, distinguished face.

43

THE MOONSTONE

FOUR MINUTES PAST ONE.
They arrived breathless on the landing once more, and Lizzy ran into the drawing room. The eerie light from the low moon hanging over the roof of the stables flooded in through the huge bay window as she rushed to draw the curtains.

Darkness.

This is the final chance! she thought, as she scanned the room for a telltale gleam.

Nothing.

She ran through the short wood-panelled passage to the spare bedroom.

Nothing but darkness.

Back down the passage towards the landing. She could just make out Josh running into the main bedroom …

Still nothing. Time was running out.

Lizzy stopped in her tracks.

At the bottom of the panelling there was a scarcely visible glimmer of light. It seemed to change colour—red, blue, green …

She frantically searched the panelling with the palms of her hands, looking for some kind of handle. Nothing.

She banged against it in frustration and it gave a fraction, then sprang back as a catch was released and a small door creaked open.

Stooping, Lizzy entered the priest's hole.

Although she had rehearsed it a hundred times in her head, nothing could have prepared her for this moment.

A pencil-thin moonbeam shafted through the far wall and burst into rainbow shards of brilliant light as it hit the huge diamond on its stand, sending swirling patterns of multicoloured radiance into the long narrow gap between the walls. As the beam moved slowly towards its centre the Moonstone caught fire with an intensity that made Lizzy gasp. It was alive with light.

Lizzy stood staring, open-mouthed, mesmerised by the burning gaze of this alien eye. Then the beam moved past the centre and the fires gradually died down. The Moonstone loosened its grip on her as the light faded … It had almost gone when Lizzy heard a noise behind her. She turned …

Shankar appeared at the open doorway. He flicked on a landing light.

"Josh!" Lizzy shouted at the top of her voice, and wrenched the Moonstone from its stand. Shankar was upon her in an instant, grabbing her arm and forcing the diamond from her hand. As she stood panting in front of him, he looked at her triumphantly.

"Thank you, my dear!" he murmured with an ice-cold smile. "Finally."

"But it's got to go back to the Temple," Lizzy said desperately.

"You foolish child," Shankar said, shaking his head. "I have far bigger plans for it than that."

Something Alison had told Lizzy at school about overexcited dogs suddenly sprang into her mind—"Kick 'em in the balls, Lizzy!" she'd said. "It works for men too!"

Lizzy lashed out, kicking Shankar with all her strength between the legs, and as he doubled up Josh scrambled into the priest's hole and rugby-tackled him from behind, sending him sprawling. The Moonstone skittered across the parquet floor—Josh hung onto Shankar's legs, shouting "Run, Lizzy! Run!"

She grabbed the diamond, shoved it into her pocket and bolted across the landing into a bedroom. She heard quickening footsteps behind her as Shankar gave chase.

Ducking into a bathroom, then a dressing room, she threw open a door, then another. Slamming them all behind her, she sprinted for the back staircase, glancing back and glimpsing Shankar in pursuit, his black eyes glinting with a fanatical fury.

Lizzy darted up the stairs and into the attics. Stumbling through room after room full of old luggage and broken furniture, she sensed Shankar had lost sight of her. Moonlight filtered through the skylights and the distant sounds of music and laughter echoed through the corridors.

She turned a corner and paused to catch her breath; tiptoeing into another room to find a place to hide she was terrified by the sight of the enormous stuffed python hanging on the wall. Suppressing a scream, she ran out into the corridor but Shankar saw her from the other end. Just beside her there was a small trapdoor leading onto the roof, and Lizzy scrambled through. Shankar grabbed her by the ankles and tried to drag her back in. Kicking out furiously she just managed to get free.

"It's mine, damn you!" he swore, struggling through the trapdoor as she jumped to her feet in the gutter between two sloping roofs. At the end she turned, running along a narrow stone parapet, the brilliant moon lighting her way. Shankar was catching up. Down below the party guests, alerted by Josh, streamed onto the terraces, pointing up and shouting. She ran down another gulley, and then realised it led to a dead end. She was trapped! Shankar started to close in slowly ...

She scrambled desperately up the skiddy roof slates, just managing to pull herself to her feet at the top by a chimney ...

There was a yawning drop between her and the parapet of another wing of the house.

"Lizzy!" she heard Henry's voice from below.

She gritted her teeth and made a huge effort ...

The onlookers gasped with horror as they saw her leap, flying across the gap, stumbling on the narrow stone ledge as she landed perilously close to the edge.

The huge dome of Shalimar loomed above her, all its colour drained by the moonlight. The tumble had cut her forearms and head, and blood ran down her face. Shankar was gazing down at her like a tiger preparing to pounce.

An old wooden ladder lay abandoned in the roof gutter. Grabbing it, Lizzy propped it against the railings of the balcony surrounding the bottom of the dome and scurried up. One of the rotten rungs near the top snapped under her weight and splinters tore into her hands as she hung on for dear life, her feet flailing around for a foothold. She finally managed to get her shoe onto a rung and made the last few steps to the balcony rail ...

She was just in time. She felt the ladder sway under her feet as Shankar snatched it away, and she pulled herself over the railing, landing in a heap on the narrow balcony. An iron door in the wall supporting the dome was rattling furiously. She ran over and pulled desperately at the handle. The door was rusted solid.

"Lizzy!" she heard her father shout from the other side.

"Dad!"

They were an inch apart but it might as well have been a million miles.

Shankar's face appeared over the balcony rail.

As he climbed over and moved towards her Lizzy ran round the balcony to the far side of the dome. Shankar chased her, swearing under his breath. She just managed to stay out of his clutches as they ran round and round, dodging one way, then the other.

The iron door shuddered from heavy kicks—they were trying to break through … If she could only keep Shankar at bay!

Then she spotted the metal rungs. They were set into the wall and ran up over the smooth overhanging bulge of the copper dome. Lizzy scrambled up them as fast as she could. She had to heave herself over the bulge, her hands horribly painful as she hung on.

As she rounded the overhang she could hear Shankar panting below. Lungs bursting, she used the rungs to slide herself up the copper roof, hauling herself towards the decorative crown. She looked back and the huge drop to the ground swam before her eyes. If she slipped now, there was nothing to hold her …

At the top of the dome a high metal pole spearing a globe and surmounted by a full moon thrust up towards the starry night sky. Lizzy clutched on to it—there was nowhere else to go. She watched in terror as Shankar heaved himself over the lip of the roof.

Slowly but inexorably he climbed towards her, pulling himself towards the crown. Desperately trying to stamp on his hands she nearly lost her footing, leaving her swinging from the metal pole. Screaming in agony, legs thrashing in mid-air, she just managed to scramble back to her feet.

Then she saw Peregrine on the roof way below!

He was sitting cross-legged with his back to her on a little railed platform overlooking the Mughal garden, gazing at the full moon, oblivious to what had been happening behind him.

Suddenly it was blindingly clear to Lizzy what she had to do.

Reaching into her pocket, she pulled out the Moonstone and waved it in front of Shankar, taunting him as he snatched at it. He watched the enormous diamond intently. So near, but so far ...

"Peregrine!" she shouted at the top of her voice. He turned, and Lizzy tossed the Moonstone in a great arc through the night sky towards him. As it flew past Shankar he desperately tried to grab it, losing his grip on the dome. He slid faster and faster down the smooth copper.

Shankar's screams filled the air as he finally slipped over the lip of the dome and disappeared from sight. Lizzy heard a crash of breaking glass ...

The remaining guests in the Durbar Hall looked up in horror as Shankar shattered the skylight high above their heads and plunged, arms flailing as if in slow motion, face down onto the candelabra, his body impaled by dozens of the stainless-steel flames. Blood and candle wax splattered the guests' dinner jackets and ball-gowns as they recoiled in revulsion, tripping over each other in their panic. Shankar writhed in agony on the swaying candelabra …

The chains holding it groaned under the extra weight. One snapped, then another, then the last two, and it plunged to the floor with a resounding clang.

Shankar twitched, then lay still. He was dead.

44

MORE SUPRISES

"THANK GOD—YOU'RE SAFE!" her father said, as he reached up and took Lizzy's hand.

"Is Shankar … you know?" she asked him as he helped her down onto the balcony. He nodded as he hugged her tight with relief.

Henry had finally managed to prise the iron door open with the help of Josh just in time to see Shankar flying over his head and falling through the skylight. He had glimpsed him spreadeagled on the candelabra below and turned away sickened, then blocked the view to prevent Josh from looking down too.

"Have you still got it?" Josh began to ask, but Lizzy suddenly started shaking, and sat down heavily.

Peregrine appeared through the door and knelt before her.

"Th … the … ?" she stammered.

"It was like plucking the moon itself from the sky," he answered, so quietly that only she could hear.

He helped her to her feet, and they all went back through the iron door. While her father led the way down through the interior of the dome and Josh followed, Peregrine held Lizzy back for a moment.

"I've hidden the Moonstone," he whispered.

"How did you know … ?" Lizzy looked at him in astonishment.

"Never mind. I've made a study of such things. And we both know what should happen to it, don't we?"

"Lizzy?" Henry's voice called up the steep wooden stairs.

"Just coming," Peregrine replied for them both. He clasped her hands, and looked at her earnestly. "For now, only you and I know I have the Moonstone—"

"It's got to go back to the Temple of the Moon," Lizzy said without hesitation.

A smile broke through Peregrine's usually inscrutable expression. "So it should, and I can help make sure it does. But if William and Lavinia get their hands on it … "

"They musn't," Lizzy stated simply.

"Then here's what we must do." He quickly murmured his plan, and Lizzy nodded her agreement.

They all stumbled down the back stairs to the hallway where Chief Constable Briggs was trying to bring order to the chaos, barking commands into his mobile phone and making sure no one disturbed Shankar's body. White-faced guests were being consoled by their concerned spouses as police and ambulance sirens wailed their way up the drive to the house.

Peregrine went over to the Chief Constable and quietly told him something. His eyes narrowed, and he discreetly signalled to the sergeant who had driven him to the party. After a few words from the Chief Constable, the sergeant walked swiftly out of the house towards the Mughal Garden.

"I'd like to see everyone involved in this tragedy in the living room in fifteen minutes," the Chief Constable announced.

"Let's see if we can't get to the bottom of it."

Chief Constable Briggs leant back on his chair in the drawing room and blew out of his cheeks. "That's quite a story, young lady!"

Lizzy nodded. As they had all sat round on the sofas and chairs, she had told him slowly and clearly what had happened right from the time she had been given the journal. The only things she had left out were any mention of the curse—and the fact that Peregrine had caught the Moonstone.

"I assume that you have someone looking for this diamond, Briggs?" Lavinia asked. She had recovered her composure, although her face was still pale and drawn.

"Indeed I have," the Chief Constable responded. "It'll show up soon enough, I reckon."

"And I suppose," Lavinia continued, "that the Moonstone must belong to William as the owner of Shalimar and heir to George Abercrombie. Is that right, Briggs?" She was already imagining herself wearing it at the ball next year—it would make up for this year's disasters. Would it be better as a brooch or a pendant, she wondered … ?

"It is, yes."

"It should go back to India, to where it belongs," Peregrine stated forcefully.

"Hear, hear!" came a woman's voice from by the door.

Everyone turned in surprise.

"Rose!" exclaimed Henry. "Where have you been?"

She'd been listening unnoticed for quite some time, and seized the moment. Quietening Henry with a gesture, she spoke directly to the Chief Constable. Her tangle of brown hair tumbled untidily onto her denim jacket

"You're certain that the Moonstone belongs to the owner of Shalimar?" she asked.

"That's right. The heir of—"

271

"Of course he's sure, you silly girl," Lavinia interrupted. "It's mine ... ours, I mean."

"In that case," said Rose in a voice that was calm and deadly serious, "it's all the more important that you should know that this evening I have finally uncovered proof that Henry is the rightful heir of Shalimar ... and, so it would seem, of the Moonstone too!"

Pandemonium burst out—accusations and insults flying thick and fast until the Chief Constable managed to calm things down.

"What do you mean by this, young woman?" he asked sternly.

"You shouldn't ask me ... " Rose replied, opening the door. A neatly dressed elderly woman stepped out of the shadows. "Ask her instead!"

"Mabel Corker!" Lizzy and Josh both blurted out. William went deathly pale.

"That's right, Mabel Corker," Rose repeated, nodding at Lizzy and Josh. "I overheard you two talking about her and the name rang a bell. Turned out she'd once been a friend of my aunt's." Lizzy looked at Josh, puzzled. She couldn't remember a situation when they might have been overheard ...

Mabel walked briskly into the middle of the room. Taking a long drag on her cigarette she surveyed the assembled company. Her gaze lingered fondly on Henry for a moment, then she remembered what she had come to do.

"I have a confession to make," she announced in her husky voice.

William jumped to his feet. "This is outrageous!" he blustered. "Briggs, I will report you to your superiors if you listen to a word this impostor says ... "

"My superiors, eh?" the Chief Constable observed quietly. "You might find that difficult, Mr Abercrombie. There's no one higher up than me in the police force of North Yorkshire."

William continued protesting, but the Chief Constable silenced him. "I could always ask my officers to arrest you for obstructing an investigation, Mr Abercrombie, if that's what you want. Now, let's hear from—" he looked at his notes—"Mabel Corker, is it?"

Mabel nodded, and told her story. It was Lizzy's turn to be glued to her seat.

Mabel recounted how, as their future nanny, she had been present at the birth of William and Henry, and, at the same time, the tragic death of their mother. The doctor in attendance wasn't the family doctor, who was on holiday, but his junior partner, Dr Critchley. He'd noted the details of the twins' births on a piece of paper and sent Mabel off to Knowlesby to register the births—and Fenella's death.

"It was all terribly upsetting," Mabel said. "I was so fond of Mrs Abercrombie … "

She'd been fired for stealing when the twins were six— she was sure William had planted the silverware in her bedroom cupboard—and had gone to work in a hotel in Harrogate. Years later she'd seen a copy of *Tatler* magazine with photographs of William's marriage to Lavinia. They reminded her that she still had a few mementoes from her Shalimar days, and there, at the bottom of the shoebox containing them, she'd found the crumpled note that Dr Critchley had written: "Dark-haired, brown-eyed boy, William, born 5.23 pm, blond, green-eyed boy, Henry, born 5.28 pm."

"But William's blond and I'm dark … " Henry frowned, not understanding. Rose shushed him …

For the first time Mabel had realised that in her distraught state she had made a terrible mistake when she registered the twins. She'd found Dr Critchley in York, and he'd remembered the births very well, and had confirmed from memory what he'd written on his note.

Then—Mabel paused dramatically before she continued—she'd come to Shalimar to tell William about her blunder but he had first threatened her, and then offered to buy her silence.

"William?" Lavinia looked at him, horrified. He glared at Mabel defiantly.

"Go on … " the Chief Constable encouraged her.

"What was I to do?" Mabel pleaded, wringing her hands. "I'm a poor woman, with no pension to speak of … " She choked back a sob. "He paid me off handsomely for a while, then a few years back I got him to set me up in the best nursing home in Knowlesby, with plenty of pocket money for my little … habits."

"When did all this start?" the Chief Constable asked.

"Fifteen years ago. A few months after they were married … "

Henry looked at his brother, aghast. "You've known all this time, William?"

William scowled furiously as everyone looked at him in disgust. "You'll never get away with this, Henry," he exploded. "I'll throw the pair of you out of Maya Lodge, and to hell with you both!"

"William!" Lavinia looked appalled.

"That's what he said he'd do when I told him I knew Mabel," Lizzy burst out, and she explained what happened on their visit to the nursing home. "No wonder he paid for me to go Laythorpe! To get me away!"

Henry had turned ashen white. "And I thought it was generosity on your part," he said, gazing at William sadly. He'd never suspected that his brother could be so wicked …

"I'll fight you through every court in the land!" William spat the words out viciously.

Only the Chief Constable remained unperturbed. "I wouldn't if I were you, Mr Abercrombie," he advised him calmly. "I've heard enough tonight to arrest you right now on suspicion of obtaining money and property by deception. You should get a nice prison term when you're found guilty. Unless of course—" he raised an eyebrow—"your elder brother chooses not to press charges."

William deflated like a balloon.

"How could you do this to us, William," Lavinia sobbed. "What will the Sams say?" She threw herself face down on the sofa and burst into tears.

"Bloody 'ell, so much for my nice evening off!" the Chief Constable mumbled to himself, as the sergeant knocked on the door. "Yes, Hardcastle, what is it?"

"Beggin' your pardon, sir, but we haven't had much luck … "

"Keep trying, sergeant. I'll join you in a mo … "

The Moonstone had almost been forgotten during all these startling revelations, and Chief Constable Briggs closed his notebook. "I'll need to interview you all individually," he said. "But first off, it looks like I'd better supervise the search."

They all started talking at the same time as he left, but Rose seized everyone's attention again. "It's not my place to say so," she said, "but I'm sure that no one would now argue with Peregrine's suggestion that once it is recovered the Moonstone should be returned to the temple in India."

Peregrine nodded his approval, while Henry looked in amazement at Rose, admiring and adoring her equally. Lizzy was ashamed of the doubts she'd had about her; not only had she restored her father's birthright, she too wanted the Moonstone to go back to India.

"It's got to go back," Lizzy told her father quietly. "We've got no choice."

"What do you mean?" he asked.

"The Moonstone. It's the cause of the curse." She looked at her father intently as the full significance of what she had said slowly dawned on him.

"You knew about the curse?"

"Yes. It killed Mum." She had a lump in her throat.

"Is that why you did all this?" he asked gently.

Lizzy nodded.

"Then you are as wise as you are brave, Lizzy. You confronted the past and, thanks to you, now we all have a future … "

A huge weight had been lifted from both their shoulders. Henry glanced longingly at Rose.

The Chief Constable returned, looking puzzled; they hadn't yet been able to find the diamond, but he was sure they would in due course … As the conference broke up, everybody talked to everyone else about the extraordinary events of the evening. Lavinia stormed off to her bedroom, followed by William who kept trying to justify his actions to her …

Henry and Mabel's reunion was emotional for both of them. Even though he couldn't recall much detail, he remembered well the strong feeling that he had once had for her.

"I always thought William was a wrong 'un," she confided, "and I'm glad that it's all out in the open now."

Rose drove her back to Knowlesby, and when she returned Henry and her went out onto the terrace and sat on a bench. Dawn was starting to tinge the eastern sky.

"I don't know how to thank you, Rose." He took her hand in his.

"You don't need to," she replied, resting her head upon his shoulder.

"How did you come to find this all out … ?"

"It's a long story … "

"I can imagine!"

"When I overheard Lizzy and Josh talking about this Mabel Corker who'd been your nanny, I remembered that my aunt had mentioned her from time to time. There can't be two with a name like that, can there? My aunt used to live in Harrogate and had been a friend of hers."

"Quite a coincidence, my nanny knowing your aunt … "

"Yes, but that's only the start. When I spoke to her about Mabel, my aunt remembered that she had once hinted that she had a hold over someone who helped her financially. Mabel talks too much when she had a drink or two, as I later found out."

"Anyway, they lost touch when my aunt moved to London, and that would have been that, but Lizzy had mentioned the fact that William was paying for Mabel to live at the nursing home, and I put two and two together—"

"You mean, you figured out that I was really the elder?"

"No, not at that stage. But I reckoned that it had to be something pretty serious for William to be paying for her—and keeping it secret from you. Then it was a matter of getting Mabel to admit it all … that's what took so long."

"You are amazing. How on earth did you persuade her?"

277

"She's a lonely, talkative woman and at the end of the day, she is still very fond of you. But it was only yesterday that she finally told me about the birth certificate—"

" Yes, you told me you had important news."

"But I couldn't tell you what until I was absolutely sure. I managed to track down Dr Critchley at a dinner in Leeds earlier this evening—"

"That's why you missed the Ball?"

"Yes. I took Mabel with me and he confirmed every word of what she'd told me. Then I came straight here—and found all this going on. The rest you know."

Henry shook his head in wonder and looked at Rose passionately. "You've made this the most remarkable day of my life," he said, "but there's one thing that would ensure that I will remember it for ever … Will you marry me?"

Rose looked at him and smiled. "Yes, I will."

Lizzy was delighted to hear the good news, and she and Peregrine had a chat in the library. He suggested that it would be safe to trust Rose and her father with the secret of the Moonstone, but that it shouldn't go further than them.

"But I've got to tell Josh!" Lizzy exclaimed. "I'd never have got it without him … "

Peregrine looked at her doubtfully.

"I'd trust him with my life," she answered the unasked question.

"All right, Lizzy, it's your decision. But please, no one else after him. Can you imagine if the press got hold of the story? They'd have a field day, and then museums and governments would get involved. The Moonstone would never be allowed back to the temple."

Lizzy nodded. "Where did you hide it?" she asked.

"In the jaws of the python." He laughed when she pulled a face. "Very appropriate, in fact. In India, the snake is a symbol of the moon."

45

RETURN TO INDIA

THE RAJA OPENED the rusty iron gateway into the neglected gardens and ushered them through. He was far less cold than the last time Lizzy had met him, but then his feelings about George Abercrombie had been changed by what she had told him.

Peregrine walked in ahead and quickly took in the surroundings. Rose and her father followed, more absorbed in each other than anything else. They'd only married the week before, and it had been Lizzy's idea to make their secret trip to India their honeymoon.

She looked around her. The huge rectangular gardens were surrounded by high walls, with crumbling white-marble pavilions overlooking empty ponds and overgrown pathways. The lawns where once peacocks had strutted were tangled with weeds, and a mangy dog snuffled in the undergrowth. The dazzling hot sun beat down. She took off her hat and wiped her forehead.

"You want the Pool of Rainbows?" the Raja asked, and Lizzy nodded wearily.

It had been an exhausting two months since Shankar's death. Her father had mostly managed to keep Lizzy's role in it out of the press, but the adjourned inquest and all the ructions with Uncle William over Shalimar had been very stressful. The Chief Constable had forbidden anyone from talking publicly about the Moonstone until it was found. Mabel Corker had mysteriously disappeared, a descendant of George's son Krishna had apparently been found, and on top of it all her father had married Rose—and Lizzy had been the maid of honour!

She was tired too from their stay in Mumbai where KK had laid on lavish entertainment every day—his way of making some sort of amends for having introduced Shankar to the Abercrombie family with fatal consequences ...

But it had been fun to see Kiva and Johnny Cairo again, and Lizzy had gone on his motorbike for a tour of Malabar Hill. Through the trees there she'd glimpsed the Towers of Silence where the Parsees lay out their dead to be eaten by vultures. Strange—once she would have thought it was a horrible thing to do, but now she found it no different from leaving people to be eaten by worms in an English graveyard ...

"Here we are!" cried the Raja, bringing her back to the present. They climbed down the narrow marble steps into a large mildew-stained marble chamber open to the sky.

"I want you all to sit down here and close your eyes," Lizzy explained, pointing to the rim of the dried-up marble pool. Taking the printout of Uncle George's journal from her pocket she added, "And imagine it's one night, a hundred and fifty years ago ... "

She read aloud.

After a few years I had risen steadily in the Honourable East India Company's service, and attended the coronation of Nawab Mahabatkhan II in Junagadh, an independent state over which the

Company was keeping a watchful eye. The Nawab was only eleven, and the real power rested in the hands of his mother, the Regent, who saw the advantage to be gained from having an Englishman on the inside, and fixed on me for the execution of her plan.

*The coronation celebrations were held near the fort overlooking the city, in the Shalimar Gardens. Shalimar! The very name evokes its meaning in Sanskrit—*The Abode of Love!*Even now I can remember every detail of that fateful night—the scent of roses and almond blossom hanging in the still, warm air; the blaze of stars like crushed diamonds across the sky; those haunting Indian melodies and delicate silk-clad dancing girls; the torch lights reflected in the waters of the marble ponds where hundreds of fountains played— my senses were already intoxicated when the Regent suggested that I should see the Pool of Rainbows. She bade me follow her, and led me to the marble entrance, then with a strange smile, left me to go in alone.*

I descended the narrow stairs, and gazed around me in wonder. If man has ever devised a more beautiful place, I can't imagine it. Water streamed down three sides of the marble room and scores of oil lamps in the niches behind glowed with the softest of lights. The spray from the water falling into the pool at the bottom filled the air, dissolving the lamplight into a thousand rainbows. And into this delirious beauty walked Leela—her fine, dark eyes locked with mine, and love struck in that instant. Her dark hair framed a face of such sweetness and tender feeling that I reached out and gently placed my hand upon her soft cheek—she blushed in confusion, as a high-born Indian lady must, and retreated, but not without giving me the shy backward glance which sealed my fate.

"So it really was a love match," sniffed the Raja, dabbing his eyes with a handkerchief. Rose and her father held hands, visibly moved.

Peregrine shook his head sadly. "Thank you, Lizzy," he murmured quietly.

"Thank you," Lizzy replied. Without his help none of their trip would have been possible. He had understood all that she wanted to do, and why.

As they made their way out they passed through a ruined pavilion at one end of the gardens.

"He lived here with Leela," Lizzy told them, "and their son, Krishna."

But all that was before Uncle George stole the Moonstone ...

Through an arched window they could see whitewashed temples glinting in the sunlight high above on the cliffs of Girnar Mountain. And somewhere up there was the cave, too, Lizzy thought.

46

THE TEMPLE OF THE MOON

T HE STONE FLAGS in the courtyard of the Temple of the Moon still retained the heat of the day when they arrived shortly before sunset. The Raja had stayed behind in Barvela—he had not been invited. The evening's ceremony was to be secret to all but a select few.

First Lizzy wanted to lay another ghost to rest.

As they took their shoes off before they went in, she suggested that Rose, Peregrine and her father sat down and listened to another extract from the journal. It was the one she knew only too well: '*I decided to visit the Temple of the Moon at nearby Somnath to witness the full-moon ceremony ...*' As she read on, Lizzy glanced around the courtyard, as if she might glimpse her uncle in the lengthening shadows. The story unfolded— the earthquake, the buried idol, the Moonstone ...

Without a moment's hesitation I took my clasp knife and gouged out the diamond and, ignoring the moans of the injured and dying, left the temple, mounted my horse and rode off in the moonlight to Veraval. Not one person had witnessed my actions in that evil hour.

She slowly folded the printout and put it back in her pocket.

"Who would have thought that a single rash act could have such dreadful results?" Lizzy's father whispered, shaking his head sorrowfully. For generations his family had been blighted by that moment of madness.

"You think doing something on the spur of the moment somehow relieves us of our responsibility for it?" Peregrine answered. "I think not." It was almost as if he were thinking aloud.

Rose looked at him, intrigued. Despite all the time they'd spent with Peregrine in India, he remained as mysterious as ever. "It's odd, isn't it?" she mused. "The Curse never killed Uncle George even though he was the one who actually stole it … "

"Yes, but it blighted his life," Lizzy replied.

"What?" Rose smiled at Lizzy sceptically. "Married an heiress who adored him, and lived at Shalimar? Some blight! … "

At that moment two skinny Brahmin priests wearing loose ochre-coloured robes with brocaded borders came out of the temple.

"Mr Coates?" one asked in immaculate English, looking back and forth between Peregrine and Henry.

"I am Peregrine Coates." He bowed in greeting.

"Raman Pujari. Shankar was my cousin. This is my brother, Prakash."

Lizzy shuddered as the other Brahmin nodded amiably. Even though Peregrine had warned her she would meet Shankar's relatives, she hadn't expected to feel so awkward—guilty, almost.

"Is this the young lady?" Raman asked. Peregrine nodded.

The Brahmin looked at Lizzy with his intense dark eyes. "We owe you a debt of thanks which can never be repaid," he stated simply. He put his hands in prayer in front of him, and made a low bow. Lizzy was overwhelmed; she felt unbelievably honoured. "The Pujari family have been priests of this temple since time immemorial," he continued. "You can imagine our shock when we heard that the Moonstone had been tracked down in England—we and thousands of pilgrims believed we were worshipping in front of it every day of every year, with no idea that our sacred diamond was a fake."

"You must have been horrified," Henry murmured.

"It was made all the worse by the knowledge that years ago, before he was expelled from the brotherhood, Shankar had tried to convince the elders that he had found evidence that our so-called Moonstone was a glass replica, but at first they ignored him, then he was found trying to break into the archives, they became convinced that he was dangerously obsessed."

"So Shankar was right … " Peregrine said.

The priest shrugged. "Right about the Moonstone, yes. But when he was expelled, he vowed to track it down for himself and swore he would destroy the Brotherhood. He was deranged!"

"He certainly was the night he was chasing Lizzy across the rooftops!" Henry said with a shiver. Rose squeezed his hand.

"It is time,"Raman said. "As you may imagine it had been very difficult to keep this ceremony secret. There are thousands of pilgrims in Somnath tonight who still expect to attend the full-moon celebration. We shall keep it, as you Britishers like to say, short and sweet."

The sun was still hovering over the horizon as the priests led them into the temple. It was empty, and the candles

287

threw long shadows on the cool marble floor. Peregrine spoke quietly to Lizzy as they crossed the temple. "You can understand now why I told you that it was as crucial for our friends the Brahmins to keep this secret as it is for us,"

She nodded. "They've been worshipping a fake for a hundred and fifty years without knowing it. If that got out … "

There was a stepladder beside the large bronze statue of a six-armed god at the back of the temple. The two Brahmins moved in front of it, chanting. Lizzy and the others followed behind.

"Is that the replica? … " Rose asked quietly, looking at the glittering yellow object in the centre of the idol's forehead.

"An exact model in glass," Peregrine said. "And practically worthless."

He reached into his pocket and whispered to Lizzy, "I think it would be fitting if you presented the Moonstone." She smiled as he put the huge diamond in her hand and squeezed it. She glanced at her father, and then at Rose who looked so lovely. She was her mother now …

"Wait!" she told Peregrine impulsively. "Let Rose do it." She went over to her and explained in a low voice what she was expected to do, handing her the Moonstone.

"That's so sweet of you, Lizzy!" Rose cried, a catch in her voice.

Lizzy watched as Rose gazed at the diamond in fascination, the reflected colours playing on her face. Although they had all marvelled at it before, seeing the Moonstone in the temple brought home the sublime mystery of it. It was shaped like two pyramids stuck together and was about the size of a billiard ball. Rose turned it slightly in her hand—and gasped as the light inside the stone suddenly disappeared and her face was plunged into darkness. She'd found the flaw! The elusive flaw that none of them had yet managed to locate!

The clattering of the stepladder drew their attention back to the idol. Prakash moved the ladder into position, climbed up and carefully removed the glass replica.

Raman continued with his incantations as Prakash climbed back down and Rose moved forwards with the Moonstone. He handed the replica to her, as Raman waved a censer billowing clouds of heavy incense in front of the idol. They stood for a moment in silent prayer then Rose presented Prakash with the diamond. Raman's chanting grew louder as Prakash mounted the ladder and restored the Moonstone to the forehead of the idol.

The chanting stopped.

"Its rightful resting place!" Lizzy thought, overwhelmed by relief. She grinned at Peregrine, who squeezed her shoulder, while her father hugged Rose.

The two Brahmins looked up at the idol impassively. The long wait was over.

Rose held the replica out and offered it silently to Lizzy.

"No, no," she insisted quickly. "Please, you keep it. I want you to."

Rose smiled as she slipped it into her bag.

"Other than the priests, we four are the only ones who know that it is the real Moonstone in the forehead of the idol once more," Peregrine explained to them as they watched the full moon rise over the Arabian Sea. "That way we will be certain that it will be safe, for who would steal a worthless piece of glass?"

289

Henry applauded at the ingenuity of it. "Hidden in full view! Whose brilliant idea was that?"

"Yes, whose?" Rose persisted.

Peregrine sidestepped the question. "But for Lizzy, none of this would have happened." He smiled as she and Rose walked on. "A remarkable girl—so like her mother."

Henry nodded slowly, and looked at Lizzy chattering away happily. He was inexpressibly proud of her.

"Alice believed implicitly in the curse," Peregrine said. "But like me, she never figured out what could be done about it. And then it was too late … "

He paused. The memory was painful for both of them.

"I always knew that the moon had something do with it," Peregrine continued, "and I tried many full-moon rituals to combat it. I even came across the story of the Moonstone in my researches, but I didn't make the connection. It took Lizzy to do that."

Henry shook his head. "I still find it incredible … "

"Ever the scientist … " Peregrine said with a faint smile. "Your field is photosynthesis, isn't it?"

Henry nodded. "But funnily enough … "

"So you know that the light of the sun brings life," Peregrine waved to where the last red stain of sunset was fading in the west. "But no one knows what the light of the moon brings."

"Actually, that's exactly what I'm working on," Henry said.

Peregrine was surprised. "I had no idea," he murmured. He had always thought that Henry's researches would be of no interest to him. *Strange how everything has changed*, he thought to himself.

"And what's the book you're working on about?" Henry asked.

"It's going to be called *Dreamtime*."

"Oh!" It was Henry's turn to be surprised. "That sounds interesting. What's it about?" he asked.

"I'm trying to paint a different picture of the Muslim world." Peregrine smiled his inscrutable smile.

"Well, it certainly sounds different ... "

They gazed silently at the full moon as it slowly climbed in the eastern sky.

"There's one more thing that Lizzy wants to do before we leave for home," Peregrine remarked after a long pause. "She hasn't told me what, and I haven't asked."

47

THE HOLY MAN

"IT'S VERY BEAUTIFUL, LIZZY," her father said as they neared the cave in the mountains. "But I still don't understand why you brought us up here."

Lizzy smiled mysteriously. "You'll see," was all that she would say.

They'd met up with the Raja at his palace in Barvela, and had been joined by Shah Mustaq Ali who had acted as their guide, on the way showing them the Asokan inscriptions on a huge flat rock at the bottom of the mountain.

"The Emperor Asoka became sickened by the bloodshed and violence of his early reign," he explained, "and over two thousand years ago he became a disciple of the Lord Buddha. Asoka caused his enlightened rules to be carved onto rocks throughout his domains and these here at Girnar were the first to be inscribed. He provided medical care for all people and animals, encouraged religious tolerance, discouraged extremism in any form, and taught respect and generosity between family, friends and acquaintances … "

"He sounds amazing, don't you think?" Rose said to Peregrine. He looked at her with his clear grey eyes.

"Yes," he replied, and turned to Shah Mustaq Ali. They talked intently about Asoka and Sufism during the long hard climb up to the cave, while the Raja engaged Rose and Henry in speculation about George Abercrombie.

Lizzy had walked on her own, wrapped up in her thoughts.

They were all relieved when the final giddy ascent of the stone staircase to the cave was over. Lizzy stayed by the entrance, drinking in the silence, while Shah Mustaq Ali showed the others the temple ruins inside.

"That was incredible!" Lizzy's father exclaimed when they all came back and sat down to rest.

The Raja had recovered some of his buoyant good humour since the sombre visit to the Shalimar Gardens, and he couldn't resist teasing Lizzy.

"So, young lady," he called, leaning on the shrine and studying the inside of the cave, "we have been talking about your wicked Uncle George. Your father tells me he murdered someone in his London club. Damn bad form, I'd say! I hope they blackballed him!"

"On the contrary, it seems they covered up for him ... " Henry murmured.

"Uncle George disappeared," Lizzy told the Raja.

"So I hear. I don't suppose that you know where he went?"

"I do actually," Lizzy said. All eyes turned to her.

"Where?" asked the Raja.

"You're sitting on his grave!"

The Raja sprang off the shrine as if he had received an electric shock.

"You're joking, surely?" he spluttered. The others laughed uneasily.

"No, I'm not," Lizzy replied, taking the printout of the journal from her pocket and unfolding it. "Listen … "

After I fled the Turkish baths, the cash with which I had thought to pay off Mavroleon was more than enough to buy a last-minute place on a steamship from London to Bombay. Assuming the role of a devout pilgrim of no particular religion, I mumbled my prayers and chanted meaningless incantations all the way across the Arabian Sea, until we arrived off the coast of Gujarat. Stealing a lifeboat in the middle of the night was simplicity itself, and soon I found myself in the back of an ox-cart heading for Barvela—and Leela.

I confess that Mavroleon had left me caught in a web of contradictions. As far as Leela was concerned—and her family—I had deserted and dishonoured her. While Mavroleon had lied to me about Leela's death, the fact remained that I had married Penelope. I resolved to reveal myself initially only to Sanjay, who had been our loyal servant all through my marriage to Leela.

I tracked him down in Barvela. He fell to his knees when I told him who I was, and a most touching scene ensued. It was as if I had come home. Only it wasn't home; far from it. There was no way he could break it to me gently—Leela had poisoned herself when Mavroleon had shown her the announcement in The Times of my marriage to Penelope … But I had only agreed to marry Penelope because Leela was already dead, surely?

Suddenly, the magnitude of Mavroleon's villainy became clear. He had convinced me that Leela was dead when in fact she was alive, and had convinced me that she was alive when in fact she was dead. In the first case, it was so he could have her to himself, and in the second, to exact the highest price for his fiendish blackmail.

"Zar, zan, zamin," are the cause of all troubles, so they say in Urdu—money, women, land …

Do we need an excuse to go mad? If so, I had it. A perfect, textbook excuse. An ancient curse, a lost love—and Mavroleon. Even in death he thwarted me—I couldn't go back to England now, guilty as I was of his murder.

I fell into a delirium through which Sanjay nursed me. That good man believed all that I told him about Mavroleon and added that he had plagued Leela after my departure to England but she had remained steadfast and true. Even in that the villain had lied! Sanjay also told me that I was in mortal danger from Leela's family who believed me to have caused her death and would surely avenge themselves if they knew I had returned.

An outcast in India and a wanted man in England! What was I to do? I don't know when the idea first occurred me, but as soon as the seed was sown it took root. It is a tradition in India for men in old age to renounce the world, to leave their families and friends and wander the earth, surviving on the generosity of others. Young as I was, I would follow that tradition, I decided, and perhaps in that way atone for the sins that greed and folly had led me to commit. I gave my remaining money to Sanjay and retreated to this cave in the mountains where the ancients built a temple and their prayers seem to be carved into the very rocks.

At first I was afraid, and used to draw seven circles around me in the dirt to ward off evil spirits when I slept. But gradually I fell under the spell of the place and the gentle ghostly echoes of its former inhabitants. People came to visit me and gave me food, and I came to be regarded as a holy man—me, a thief, wife-deserter and murderer—a holy man! I always kept silent, of course, and my visitors read into that silence the wisdom that they sought.

And tonight, with this confession as my pillow, I will sleep a long and dreamless sleep at last.

A profound sense of peace fell on the group as Lizzy finished her reading. No one spoke, but there was nothing left unsaid. The bleating of a distant goat echoed round the cliffs.

The Shalimar curse had finally been laid to rest, and they could return to live there in peace.

48

IN FLIGHT

THE NIGHT FLIGHT was halfway back to London, the engines whining and air-conditioning hissing softly. The cabin lights had been extinguished. Uncle Peregrine and her father were still sleeping when Lizzy stirred under her blanket, and opened her eyes to see Rose contemplating the replica diamond under her reading light, the reflected rainbow colours playing on her face as she turned it in her hand.

There was a curiously hard expression in Rose's eyes, an expression that Lizzy hadn't seen before, and it gave her an unexpected shiver up the spine. Then suddenly, as Rose revolved the stone, it was if the lights had gone out inside it.

Lizzy stifled a horrified gasp, and as Rose turned to look at her, she snapped her eyes shut.

DIANA DE GUNZBURG was born in Pakistan and is Anglo-Russian-Afghan. Her great-grandfather was the last man to be publically hanged in British India for making war on the Crown. Diana was brought up between the North West Frontier—where her father still farms his estate—and her mother's native Yorkshire. By the age of seventeen she had already made the six thousand mile journey overland between the two countries three times. She has recently published articles about her family history in *Alef* magazine and *Afghan Scene*. She lives with her husband and teenage daughter in Paris where she teaches yoga. *The Moonstone Legacy* is her first book.

Why is the relationship between the British and India so enduring? Yorkshireman TONY WILD explored the subcontinent as a young man, and started to answer that question with his popular histories for HarperCollins—*The East India Company: Trade and Conquest from 1600* (1999), *Remains of the Raj* (2001), nominated as Jan Morris' Book of the Year and the best-selling *Black Gold: A Dark History of Coffee*. A one-time actor, filmmaker and screenwriter, *The Moonstone Legacy* collaboration is his first novel.